THE LONELY WAR
OF WILLIAM PINTO

THE LONELY WAR

OF WILLIAM PINTO

[by Diana Huss Green]

An Atlantic Monthly Press Book

BOSTON   Little, Brown and Company   TORONTO

ATLANTIC–LITTLE, BROWN BOOKS
ARE PUBLISHED BY
LITTLE, BROWN AND COMPANY
IN ASSOCIATION WITH
THE ATLANTIC MONTHLY PRESS

Published simultaneously in Canada
by Little, Brown & Company (Canada) Limited

PRINTED IN THE UNITED STATES OF AMERICA

To Miss Anna Steinberg of The Boston Public Library
and to Mr. Edward C. Holmes of Conway, New Hampshire,
my appreciation and gratitude

D. H. G.

THE LONELY WAR
OF WILLIAM PINTO

⌐ Chapter I ⌐

INSIDE the spare Connecticut schoolhouse only Master Eaton and one student stayed late. The boy hunched in the hard-back chair while his mind wrestled with Greek verbs. If only he could get through the Gospel and brush up on the fourth oration against Catiline he'd be out of this school and into Yale by fall. At least that's what the schoolmaster said, but Will Pinto couldn't let himself believe it yet. What if the master went back and found some frightful error on the examination papers and changed his mind?

Steeple bells all over New Haven began to chime. Seven o'clock. Elias Eaton looked up from Will's paper. "So late?" His dim eyes didn't quite focus.

Will held back his excitement. Anxious as he was to learn all he could, he itched to leave.

"You've made a good start, William. We can begin here tomorrow." Stiffly the master eased himself out of his chair, then turning back to Will, hesitated. "That is, if your father will allow you to continue."

Will's brows shot up in surprise. His father had willingly paid the small sum Master Eaton had asked for his brothers' preparatory lessons. "Why wouldn't he? He's pleased to have Abe and Sol at Yale."

Discomfort colored the master's face. He looked away, covered a cough. "Your father — uh — Mr. Pinto — ah-mm — spoke to me, very politely, certainly, about your brother Solomon's report of our daily pledge to the King."

Will felt his own face redden. Surely his father, fanatic about the British as he was, understood. Everyone knew that in the forty years Eaton had been master here he hadn't changed so much as a quill in the schoolroom. He recited his daily allegiance as absentmindedly as he watered the plants on the windowsill. Well did Will remember his father's incredulity, and his words, "Eaton's only answer was the school has always pledged itself to the King. Unbelievable. He doesn't seem to know times change. I doubt he's even heard of the Stamp Act and if he has he likely considered it reckless gossip." There had been a thoughtful pause before his father added, "Still a fine teacher, excellent."

"It's all been forgotten," the boy said, reassuring himself and his teacher.

"Perhaps." The thin face remained clouded. "I — I'm not sure. There are others, a few more lately . . . Sometimes I —"

This lust for war was beef-witted enough, Will

thought irritably. Not that he dared disagree with his father and brothers when they returned from their endless meetings complaining loudly — the British did this, the King that. He could only listen and secretly wonder if the schoolmaster wasn't right. George III was hardly the wisest king, but there was always hope for his successor. And surely a few pennies of added tax was no reason for violence. Nor, he thought angrily, was it reason to scare a helpless old man with timeworn loyalties. He wanted to reach out, touch the narrow shoulder, tell him he had nothing to fear. But Elias Eaton was still master. Will could only hint, "I'll ask my father this night. He'll be glad enough of your help, sir. You'll see."

Master Eaton nodded. Then, "One thing more, William. You know," again that cough, "you must work hard at Yale. Your behavior must be above reproach."

"Yes, sir. I won't let you down." His excitement rose again and with it his urge to be gone.

"I mean," the man held him, "perhaps work harder, be more correct than the others."

Will's agreement was too quick.

"You *do* understand my meaning?" The dim eyes sharpened.

Yes, Will understood, was even grateful for Eaton's concern. He had been chastised more than once for being goaded into a fight. "That's all then, sir?"

"Um."

Will rose. " 'Night, sir." He headed for the door.

"Good night, William. And Will — "

The boy turned back.

"I'm proud of you. 'Tisn't often I can recommend a boy your age to Yale College. Not quite fourteen, is it?"

"Fourteen two days ago. April nineteenth."

"And it was just two days ago I marked your examination — April 19, 1775 — a good day indeed." A smile warmed his eyes. His voice softened, "I shall miss you, my boy."

"Yes." Will turned away quickly from the sadness that welled up in the old man's eyes. He wasn't accustomed to seeing emotion in that stern old Yankee face. It embarrassed Will and he moved quickly to the door. There he hesitated.

"Yes, Will?"

"Master Elias Eaton — thank you." Will flung open the door and ran.

The night air stung against his cheeks. It was done. With any luck, by fall he'd be with Abe and Sol every day. The thought sent him flying faster. He ducked in and out among the shadows of elm and maple, jumped a trough in his path, and knocked on a wooden post for luck. His father would be waiting in the kitchen with Abigail, Will's stepmother. Abe and Sol should be there too.

He darted round the corner onto Chapel Street and stopped dead. The square was always deserted at this hour, but ahead of him a torch glared. Another flame bobbed along Elm Street. The rumble of voices followed the path.

Men appeared from darkened doorways and black

alleys. About twenty, he judged. The torches lighted and shaded them to outlines. Heads were thrust forward and shoulders angled to an ominous set. There was an edgy tone to their voices and their boots scraped loudly on the cobblestones.

Cautiously, Will moved forward. He could not see any faces nor distinguish words, but their temper was clear.

Now four blazing flames darkened the night around. Anger made the air so heavy it pressed against the boy's face. The air of lawlessness emanating from the mob should have hurried him homeward but it held him. Now the words came more clearly.

"— redcoats —"

"— rotten royalists —"

Cold edged along his arms as he strained to hear.

"— shooting in Massachusetts — means war —"

"— get the Tories —"

Incoherent, disjointed words shot into the darkness while the mob waited for one of them to assume leadership. Wanting action together, afraid of it singly, they milled about.

"— Waite is one of them —"

"— should be hanged —"

"— Eaton, too —"

Will shuddered. The old teacher was so helpless in the schoolhouse.

Now at the fringe of the crowd he could distinguish forms and faces. Closest to him stood an ex-apprentice to the butcher, a wad of a boy, his body fleshed full to his pebble eyes. Next stood "Slingshot" Dunn, who spent his days blinding wharf rats for sport, and over there a pig-snouted bully named Crull. They were all here, the malcontents, the scavengers plus a handful of sailors.

"— war — that's all they'll understand —"

"— already started — we'll finish it — "

He drew back into the dark. Should he make sure Master Eaton was all right? Nonsense, as long as these men were here in the square the old man was safe. Perhaps he should stay and wait till they dispersed.

Again he studied their faces. Drifters, wastrels. For over a quarter hour he watched and listened and there still wasn't one with gumption enough to lead the others. Mr. Eaton would not be molested this night.

Finally, when his fear for the old man lessened, Will walked on. Voices followed him. "War." They caught up the word and repeated it till it hammered against his eardrums. He refused to believe it. If there had been more shooting in Massachusetts his father would still be in the shop on Long Wharf where he'd be likely to hear news quickly.

Why not see if there were any lights on the shop side of the wharf. Not a half mile out of his way. Besides he was so late already a few more minutes couldn't matter. Turning quickly he hurried onto the meadow path. It lay in darkness and he felt a flutter of hope. Surely everything was as it should be, his father home, annoyed at whatever kept Will so late.

For a moment he stood. He smelled the sea, heard the cry of the gulls and the sound of wet ropes smacking against ships' masts. Then he saw the shaft of light that cut across the fields. His stomach dropped.

He ran. Those shots in Massachusetts didn't *have* to mean war. Two, three, five more lights appeared in the countinghouses, sail lofts, warehouses and shops that lined one side of the wharf. The other side, left open for the ships, waited in shadow for the morning's activity. He heard a throb of hushed night sounds ominously different from the daytime din of the wharf. No porters shouting above the racket of the molasses kegs they rolled, no roaring dockhands, no sharp captain's curses amid the heavy clatter of mishandled cargo — only a tense murmur.

Goosebumps covered his arms. He never liked the wharf at night. It was for grown men bent on business. Suddenly he remembered. Soon he'd be at Yale, a man too, and part of it all with Abe and Sol, and his father. He grinned. He couldn't wait to tell them his news.

⌈ Chapter II ⌉

DRY GOODS
JACOB PINTO, PROP.

WILL SAW the wooden sign that jutted out above the shop door and, at the same moment, he heard them — his father, Abe and Solomon. Their voices rose excitedly. A flash of irritation burned him. Why was his father always louder than everyone else? Abraham's laughter boomed and the boy's annoyance disappeared. There's no laughter in all the colony like Abe's, he thought, as he lifted the latch and leaned in against the door.

Tonight the laugh was different. An odd timbre in it — not the unbounded delight that seemed to satisfy his entire mind and body. Puzzled by the difference, and a bit worried, Will stepped inside the shop.

Nervous shadows distorted the cloth bolts, flickered across rows of satin ribbon and the spools suspended from ceiling beams. Huge crates and kegs narrowed walking space to two corridors leading to and from the lamp in the back.

His father's voice filled the shop. "And the British had to send for reinforcements." Jacob Pinto leaned forward in the easy chair he kept at the rear of the shop for studying his ledgers. Above his silken beard his face glowed with that dark intensity Will at once loved and feared. The man's excitement charged the air. Even seated, his well-aged strength held a readiness, a will to action.

Opposite Jacob stood Abe and Sol. Both were tall and as heavily muscled as their father. But Abe was easier, less stern than Jacob, more content than Solomon. His face showed the openness of his nature while Sol's eyes were guarded.

Looking at them Will forgot about shooting and war. These three, so alike in build and thought, seemed to Will to share an invisible bond that held them together and apart from everyone else including himself.

He stood alone and unnoticed in the shadows, his hand picking at a cloth bolt until he could hold his news no longer. "I'm ready for the College," Will blurted. "Master Eaton said next term. August. With his help — you know, the lessons."

"Fine. Good work, my boy." His father looked up and smiled and put his hand out toward Will. Jacob Pinto's eyes, dark as his own, but piercing, regarded him seriously. Will's eyes switched to his brothers.

He caught a flash of angry doubt from Sol. Abe smiled, but absently. "Today is a day for rejoicing," his father said. "The War for Independence has begun. News has just come from the Massachusetts Colony. There's been a skirmish at Lexington and more fighting near Concord Village. They say —"

Jacob continued but Will only half listened. They had barely noticed his news. Even Mr. Eaton had been more excited than they were. And why was war a cause for rejoicing?

Not until he heard his father say, ". . . your brother Abraham has decided to join the militia," did Will jerk to attention. "Abe?" Abe in the war? And with their father's approval? "But he can't go. Not now." He would lose Abe even before he'd had a chance to be with him — men, together — gentlemen of the College. Anyway this war was lunacy. Why couldn't his father see that? Besides, "Abe has two more years at Yale and," the boy took a deep breath, forced himself to say what he had so long thought, "it's treason to fight against the King."

Sol slid into a wooden chair without once taking his cool gaze from Will's face. Abe leaned forward turning his head as if to make sure he heard correctly. But their father's shocked surprise flashed into anger, then as swiftly grabbed at an explanation of Will's insurgency. "I see the schoolmaster is still preaching his antiquated lessons. If only he'd manage to look beyond his books he'd soon see," Jacob's eyes hardened, "George III is a half-wit and a scoundrel." He stopped, considered a moment, went on.

"And I can see I've been mistaken in not talking to you sooner, William. But with all the meetings and work to be done here at the shop —" Jacob rose and began to pace. Three, four measured steps. Then turning to face the boy the man picked up the rhythm of his earlier tone, "Look, Will, this is our country. There is no other in the world where we've been allowed citizenship. And we're going to fight for the privilege."

"But it was the King who gave us citizenship. Besides, we're members of the Congregational Church —" Will looked desperately toward his brother. But Abe kept his face turned from them.

"Don't be a fool," Jacob thundered. Will stepped back. "The King," his father's eyes fixed him, "gave citizenship to anyone willing to work for him in the colonies. You can't believe he'd hesitate to take back his gracious gift if it wasn't to his economic advantage. As for the Church, we pay our tithes because we must. Your mother, may she rest in peace, was a communicant. I never have been." He leaned toward Will, pointing an index finger from his clenched fist. "And in spite of your mother's blood you carry the Pinto name."

Jacob would tolerate no further argument. He walked to Abe, put his arm on his shoulder and turned him around. "You are doing the right thing, Abe, the only thing you can do." Jacob's eyes lighted with fierce pride. "God's blessing."

Will looked away, trying to hide the confusion spreading inside him. His father was so sure this war was right. But Master Eaton's way made more sense. Why not endure even a scoundrel's rule to avoid bloodshed? He wanted to believe his father. Perhaps if he'd paid more attention to his talk, but then Jacob seldom discussed government matters at home. His opinions upset Will's stepmother, Abigail. Will clenched his teeth. It *was* a stupid war and now all his hopes were wasted. Abe was leaving.

"I suppose they'll send Abe to Massachusetts." Will knew his voice was testy.

"Wherever they need him, Abe wants to go." Solomon was answering the question Will meant for his father. "And so do I," he continued. "I want to enlist, too, Father."

Jacob smiled. "Not yet. Your turn will come."

Sol's eyes narrowed. "I'm just as good a shot as Abe. I can be of as much use."

Suddenly Jacob's voice was flat. "You must all leave me soon. Let it be one by one, in your proper turn."

"Perhaps they won't take Abe," Sol suggested.

Anger brought vitality back to Jacob's voice. "Soldiers are needed. Of course they will take him."

For a moment no one spoke. Even when Elias Eaton had to appear before the elders of the College to assure them that Abe was acceptable as a student, the family refused to mention the reason. What the devil was Sol afraid of now? They were freemen of the colony and had been ever since Will could remember. Will's hopes rose. But perhaps there was a chance the militia wouldn't take Abe and he'd stay on at Yale.

They'd be together. If there was even a doubt, then there was hope. Will turned quickly to his father. "May I go to the recruiting officer with Abe?" he begged.

"What a child you are, William." Jacob chuckled. "One minute you talk like a Tory and the next you're rushing to sign your brother to the opposite side."

Will flushed.

"Let him come with me tomorrow, Father. 'Twill do the boy good to meet the men he may soon be joining." Abe directed his words above Will's head.

Still smiling, Jacob nodded his assent. "Now a toast."

Will watched his father's sure movements as he took a wine bottle from the shelf. With a practiced hand he removed the cork and filled four glasses. The rich nut-flavored liquid coursed hot through the boy's throat. They drank to Abe's health. "L'chaim" — to life. "And to independence," Jacob said. Will choked. He couldn't swallow that draught. He saw Solomon eye him warily. His father and Abe took no notice. The wine reached through him to his toes. It was good to be here with his father and brothers. Their laughter was warm and full. Will could not join it. His thoughts gnawed at him.

On the Green the bare tips of the maples budded pink and the elms stirred again to tender green. The sun seemed to scent the earth with the warmth of new beginning. Nearby a clump of willows held a yellow-green promise of leaves. Will saw it all but his brother's eyes were fixed on the State House and the crowd outside it. News had spread quickly and men and boys had flocked here from New Haven itself and the towns and farms beyond. They had come on horseback, in carts, some had walked carrying their muskets with them. A few uniformed soldiers of the militia mingled among them.

Abe caught Will's arm. "There he is — Captain Baldwin, the recruiting officer." Abe spoke quietly, almost to himself. For an instant Will felt his brother hesitate. Not that Abe stopped walking — just for a second the tread of his boots sounded less certain.

A light breeze rippled through the grass. It pushed Abe's coarse linen shirt flat against taut muscles of chest and belly and billowed the sleeves and back out full. As usual, except in the coldest weather, he wore neither jacket nor jerkin and left his blouse open at the throat. His long powerful legs strode easily in plain black breeches and thick high socks. He never cared to ape the college dandy's dress and often joked with Sol about it. "You look pretty as a governor's son," he'd tease. "Me, I'm a shopkeeper's boy and it shows." Yet it was he who had inherited their father's vitality and bearing. His gait was the free step of a man who needn't think too much, so easy and sure was he of the earth he trod. Somehow just walking beside him lent Will a special importance. He took an excited extra half-step to each of Abe's.

It was a noisy group they approached, not jolly

nor angry, but with an air of purpose. Abe strode toward the officer. Will followed, dodging among the crowd. A few volunteers were richly dressed in tight knee breeches of velvet or satin, embroidered waistcoats and long silk stockings. Most wore plain broadcloth or homespun.

Abe stepped up near Captain Baldwin. Tall, lean, and hard as his brother's, this man's body held a knowledge of its own disciplined strength. He had a thin, long, English nose, a high forehead and a powerfully angled chin. His eyes were cutting as steel. Beside him stood his assistant. He was older than Captain Baldwin with a squat, thick body and a bull neck which made his head appear to thrust straight from his massive shoulders. His face was fleshy, heavy with thick skin and dull, mulish eyes. Indeed, everything about him seemed dull and heavy.

The Pintos had to wait their turn. There were several boys ahead of them. Captain Baldwin questioned each one carefully, then turned to his assistant, who slowly nodded suspicious approval. Will understood the questions had to be asked. They couldn't risk a Tory in the militia. His father had said they needed soldiers. Why must they be so careful about whom they chose?

Abe turned and smiled down at him. "Taking a little longer than we thought."

Will nodded. If Abe had the slightest doubt he would be accepted it didn't show to anyone but Will. His brother's bold features were relaxed, his body straight and proud, his arms hung at his sides. But his right thumb picked away at the edge of his middle finger.

Watching that finger work, Will's own anxiety grew. If Abe, who lived so fully by the old plain honest rules, needing no one but the father whose wisdom he accepted with the loyalty and respect that were part of these rules, if he was uncertain —

Suddenly it was their turn. Captain Baldwin waited for Abe to speak, seeming to weigh the younger man. His eyes missed nothing — not the muscular arms, the broad shoulders, the easy stance, nor the shock of black hair and brilliant dark eyes. Will's heart raced. He could not detect the slightest hint of acceptance or approval in the officer's severe lips or in those eyes that measured down from his superior position.

"I want to sign up." Abe spoke clearly.

The captain hesitated. Then, "Name?"

"Abraham Pinto."

The assistant turned to face Abe squarely. The nostrils of his broad nose stretched wider. His stare was cold. Will had seen such a look before and, as usual, it sent a tremble of anger through him.

"Son of Jacob, the merchant?" the captain asked.

"Yes, sir." Abe's thumb picked furiously but his eyes held fiercely to Captain Baldwin's and would not let go.

Time and silence held together, heavy in the air. The crowd, sensing something, not knowing what, stood closer and waited. Will heard a few shuffling feet. For a second his eye caught Eben Thompsen's but the young man, neighbor to the Pintos for as long as Will could remember, looked quickly away.

Will felt the blood rush up into his face. Abe asked no man's favors. It was his right as a freeman to fight. Hadn't he been born in this country? And Jacob before him? Hadn't they shown their allegiance to these ignorant rebels many times — on the Committee of Correspondence, in the petition to Governor Trumbull, in a hundred different ways? Will's temper flared and his face went hot. How long must they keep Abe waiting? How could he bear it?

Whatever Abraham felt he refused to lower his gaze or bend the slightest, smallest fraction of an inch.

Pride coursed fiercely through William. It was what Abe wanted, he wanted it for Abe.

It was the captain's assistant who broke the silence, a dull, frigid voice that spoke. "No Tories. No traitors. No Jew dogs neither."

A low mutter grumbled through the crowd. Indignant scarlet colored several faces. Eyes shifted. There were perplexed frowns, scowls, and lowered lids. Will waited, listened. For the first time he heard the loud silence of good men.

Abe dropped his head. With that movement the sun seemed to darken and shame cut into Will's belly like a knife. He saw Abe shiver. Stubbornness stiffened his own thin shoulders. Who were they to bend Abe's head? How dare they mock his father's house? Swift fury raced through the boy dissolving shame and caution and forcing the words from his throat.

"Abe can fight as well as any man in the colony."

Abraham's roar of laughter startled them all. "I expect the boy is right. Leastways, I can fight as well as any man signed today."

Captain Baldwin's words came as slowly and truly as his smile. "I expect you can." He stretched out his hand to Abe. "Welcome to the Tenth Company of the Seventh Regiment of the Connecticut line."

[Chapter III]

FOR THE NEXT two weeks the house bustled with preparations for Abe's departure. Jacob himself cleaned, oiled and carefully rubbed his son's musket. He ordered new boots, the finest and sturdiest, and insisted Abe allow the tailor to measure him for the uniform jacket with Connecticut's facing. But the boy was firm against tailor's breeches, so Abigail cut and sewed from cloth of her own weaving.

Watching her work selflessly from sunrise to fall, hueless as a shadow, Will wondered if she were as confused as he. She'd always retreated from any talk of war. Had she given in at last, let her pride grow, like Jacob's, fierce enough to sacrifice her flesh and blood? She was their mother's sister, who had come to care for them after their mother's death and had stayed to marry their father. Now she was gray and gaunt with straight thin lips that rarely curved up or down, and Will could not remember her any other way. She kept the larder stocked, polished the great hearthstone, scoured the pewter, and sanded the kitchen floorboards till they and she were pale. Did she have enough of herself left to think separately from, even contrary to her husband? If so, clearly she felt duty-bound to keep her opinions, as she kept her Christian religion, out of Jacob's house.

Much as Will longed to talk to someone, to try and understand why sending Abe off to war was reason for almost holiday-like preparations, he had to respect her silence.

He turned to Sol but even he seemed always busy, forever talking about Abe's departure and his own plans to follow him.

If it weren't for Elias Eaton, I couldn't stand it, he thought. He's the only one who doesn't eat, sleep and drink war. Through those last days before Abe was to leave, the lessons became a sort of respite. Master Eaton's walls shut out politics and uncertainty and closed Will in a world where answers could be found. Here one day followed logically upon the next until a fortnight had passed and Abe had gone.

It was incredible how empty he left the house, how silent it became, how time passed and Will noticed little but his brother's absence. He wasn't even aware that summer had slipped upon New Haven until one mid-afternoon in June he found himself wriggling against the dampness at the back of his shirt. From then on the heat had become heavier, pressing against his arms, his legs, his head until it was hard to think. Now, at evening, even the house seemed to sag in the still air.

He leaned over the book that lay open on the oak table in the schoolmaster's company room and struggled with the unfamiliar Greek Gospel. He was eager to finish tonight before the heat and the drone of his own voice lulled him to sleep. Even Mr. Eaton was anxious to have the lesson done with. Will noticed the old man counting the pages to the end of the chapter. Then for the sixth time Elias Eaton reread the crumpled letter in his hand. His veined forehead creased into a web of perplexed lines and behind his tiny spectacles his vague blue eyes dimmed. The creak of a board, the whisper of a breeze outside, the flicker of the tallow candle on the time-stained plaster walls were enough to draw his gaze to a different corner of the room.

A rough wooden bench stretched across the wide empty hearth. Above it hung a dark oil portrait of a solemnly dressed couple — Mr. Eaton's parents, Will guessed. The few pieces of delicate Staffordshire china, placed carefully in a crude open cabinet, seemed oddly elegant in the plain room. Glancing patterns of light drew the schoolmaster's eyes to the dishes and for a brief second he regarded them as warmly as a cherished memory. Then swiftly as a moth's wings his eyes shifted to a pair of burnished pewter candlesticks beside him. He picked one up and put it down quickly.

Will shuffled his feet and edged forward in his chair. Whatever news that letter held took all Mr. Eaton's thoughts. The old man's nervousness made it even harder for Will to concentrate. Then a noise from the back of the house sent the master scurrying out of the room.

The letter lay open on the table. Will tried to keep his eyes on his book. The minutes sounded away. Each tick of the mantel clock irritated him. "What's keeping him?" Will grumbled, angry at the schoolmaster for the temptation he had forced on him.

But the old man did not return. Will's eyes strayed toward the letter. The penmanship was all too clear. He forced his glance away but four words held him — "ask for your resignation." So that was it. Anger rose hot in his throat. He gripped the book in front of him. What right had they — Even Will's father knew the man was an excellent master. Shaking with rage and indignation the boy looked back at the letter. ". . . distort young minds . . . a traitor . . ." Will pushed himself away from the table and abruptly stood. He couldn't believe his eyes. The school overseers were severe, but still they were conservative, deliberate men. Didn't they understand? Could they really believe that harmless soul was a traitor? Will almost laughed. Those worn bones couldn't find strength, let alone appetite, for treachery. And then Will found himself reading the entire letter.

My dear sir,

I am now set down to write you on a subject which fills me and the several overseers with inexpressible concern.

As a servant of the Connecticut Colony which no longer maintains ties, either political or sentimental, with England, you have nonetheless continued outspoken loyalty to George III. Such protestation from the Schoolmaster surely will confuse, if not distort, young minds.

Since we are truly sensible of the many years' fine service you have given, we hesitate to form the appellation that would unhesitatingly be applied in the same case to another man — traitor.

However, should your present politics not be reconsidered we shall be forced to ask for your resignation.

Most sincerely yours,
OLIVER BLACKWELL, ESQ.

"There's nothing out there. I must have imagined the noise." Mr. Eaton's voice and footsteps came across the threshold simultaneously.

Startled, Will flushed. He fumbled for his chair. Suddenly a crash ripped into the room. It echoed and reechoed in the stunned silence that followed. Will's body stiffened and the back of his neck went taut. The ring of cracking glass was almost a relief. Shattered slivers hurled motion into the room as a rock shot through the window. Drunken laughter exploded outside.

The boy jumped up. Elias Eaton's face was ashen. He was unable to move.

"Where's the Tory?" someone shouted. There was

violence in the stomping boots and threatening voices.

"Come out and see if your fine king can protect you from loyal patriots."

Will recognized that voice. It was Thomas Crull, a stupid bully who had been dismissed by the schoolmaster as not worth the space he took in class. Bolstered by rum, a gang, and a cause, Crull's vengeance was unleashed. Fierce pounding shook the door. "Come out, schoolmaster, or we're coming in for you."

One glance at him and Will knew the old man was helpless. His frail body trembled and his eyes were glazed by fear.

Tory or not, Will couldn't desert him now. The boy rushed to the door, bolted it. A threatening hum vibrated through the house. Escape was impossible. "Is there a loft?" Will whispered.

"Yes, but I don't think they could miss the ladder leading to it." Mr. Eaton's face was childlike, his statement seemed a question.

"The cellar then. Where is it?" The voices outside rose to an hysterical pitch, and stones shattered the small panes of leaded glass. Mr. Eaton stood dazed. Will grabbed his arm and shook him. "Where is the cellar?"

"Kitchen." The word came out like a sob.

Half carrying, half dragging him, Will maneuvered him into the kitchen. He saw the trap door immediately and fell to his knees tugging frantically at the rusty handle. The hinges creaked hideously but the noise outside was still louder. It was impossible to see into the dark hole beneath him. Afraid to release his grip on the terrified man, Will felt about with his free arm for a ladder. "There! Come, Mr. Eaton. You'll be safe down here."

Will heard his own words and wished he could believe them. Fists thumped insanely against the door and walls. Angry shouts drummed at his ears. A thunderous impact crashed through all sound. If their wits weren't thoroughly numbed by drink the gang would surely search the cellar, Will told himself grimly.

As carefully as he could the boy helped the old man down the ladder into darkness. He had to grope for each rung. Damp coolness met them as they stepped onto the dirt floor. Will felt his way around and behind the ladder, leading Mr. Eaton by the hand. Gently he pushed the shivering man against an earthen wall. "Stay here. I'll be right back."

All at once the schoolmaster gave way. He seized Will's arm beseechingly. "Don't leave me," he pleaded. "Please, William, I beg you not to leave me."

"I must close the door and cover it."

Just as swiftly as the old man's resolution had left him it returned. Briefly his voice regained the authority of the schoolroom. "I cannot allow you to walk into a lion's den for me."

"But the Lord saved Daniel, remember?" Gently Will pried the thin fingers from his arm.

Within seconds Will was up the ladder. There was

a groan, a cracking splintering smash. No! God, no. Not inside yet. But the voices were harshly close and he could hear the quick intake of excited breathing. They were in. His head was a nightmare of throbbing fear, but he had to cover the trap door. He ran across the kitchen to the hearth. Mechanically his hand reached out and seized a braided rug. Fright blinded the sides of his eyes. All he could see was the open trap as he dragged the rug back to it. Swiftly he smoothed it over the door's hinges and as much of the rest as he could. Now he hurled himself through the small opening onto the ladder and tried desperately to pull the rug flat. His hands trembling, he eased down the door. His heart beat furiously against his heaving chest and for a second he stood clinging to the ladder while stamping thundered over his head.

Tom Crull's voice boomed through the wooden floor. "Where are you, teacher? This time *you* have a lesson to learn." He laughed drunkenly at his own joke.

"He's hiding somewhere." There was cunning in the speaker's tone. "Search the loft."

The teacher was huddled into a child's crouch where Will had left him. Will squatted beside him. "I covered the —" The sound of breaking china cut off his words. Thumping, thudding, splintering, smashing — the chilling sounds of destruction thundered above their heads. Half an hour, three quarters, or was it longer before the sounds began to diminish? An occasional thud, a last kick, a grumble.

"Aw, come on, the old man ain't here." Reluctant boots scuffed toward the door.

Will listened for the final slam. Its impact shattered some remaining glass.

"My house — my father's house." The man moaned softly beside him.

Was this the war his father had sent Abraham into? Were these his father's allies — ruffians, rabble who could torment a helpless old man and call him a traitor?

Slowly stillness returned. Mr. Eaton no longer moaned and Will realized the tension that tightened his spine and gripped at the back of his neck was fury.

His anger grew into a tight knot of rage that churned in his belly as he helped Mr. Eaton up the ladder. Tables were overturned, chairs teetered on three legs, pictures hung askew, bits of china, books and papers littered the floor.

Not until Will handed him a broom did the man seem able to move. Half dazed, he swept in front and to the right and left of where he stood, then looked at Will for direction. Will's heart twisted. He worked hard and fast. That way he didn't have to see Mr. Eaton.

At last the boy managed some order.

"Come," Will said gently, "I'll help you to bed."

The old teacher nodded gratefully.

The boy moved toward him, put his arm around the narrow shoulders and guided him to his room. Elias Eaton said nothing as Will eased him onto the bed, carefully removed shoes and stockings, dressed him in his nightshirt, and covered him with quilts. "Thank you, William." A soft sound, almost a whisper, but there was dignity in it.

Will's eyes stung. He turned and ran.

Now, at last, Will faced his father with the night's events. The careful neatness of his own home, the well-oiled furniture, the few pieces of gleaming silver somehow incensed him. And Solomon sprawled there in the big wing chair, one leg slung easily over its arm, irritated him. Sol was accepting the story too calmly. Angrily Will rubbed his hand hard against his face. His jaws hurt from clenching his back teeth together, trying to remember the respect he owed Jacob.

Abigail had gone to bed early and Will spoke freely. When he came to the part about hiding the schoolmaster, Solomon's nonchalance vanished. His eyes grew suspicious and he leaned forward in his chair. "You mean you helped a Tory?"

Will nodded, grinning inwardly. Any reaction from Sol was better than that smug disinterest he had shown. "Of course I did. The man was helpless against that mob."

"But a Tory, nonetheless." Now Sol looked anxious. "Did anyone see you leave the house?"

Will felt his neck stiffen. "I didn't have time to notice. And what difference does that make?"

Jacob, watching Will, listening to every word, had said nothing. The lines in his forehead were deep, his face shadowed by the dark beard, but his eyes shone. There was no hint of fatigue in them or his voice. "I don't care if you were seen or not. But I do care that you understand that even the best causes often attract undesirable supporters. They don't make the cause wrong. You can't believe we're proud of people like Crull and his ilk or that recruiting officer's assistant. They're so few. And they're balanced by men like the Trumbulls and John Hancock and Roger Sherman. Most people reach neither such depths nor such heights. They lie somewhere in between. Don't you see tonight's incident was more an evil of rum than the revolution? You can't honestly blame our fight for independence for what happened."

Will kicked at a chair leg. "And you can't blame it on drink," he muttered, "unless your holy war needs excuses."

Jacob's face went scarlet. He banged his fist against the table. "Of course it doesn't. But it doesn't deserve the blame for those rascals, nor will I accept blame for the school board, as surely as I've never accepted guilt for Judas's betrayal of Jesus."

A look of triumph came over Sol's face. His tone was placating, but his words held the seeds of further disagreement. "Still, we must be practical, Father. It will hardly benefit our name if news gets out that Will was seen aiding a Tory."

Jacob sighed as though suddenly tired. "Solomon, Solomon, how long will it take for you to learn I do not work for my name but for what I think right?"

For a moment Jacob looked thoughtful, then continued. "Still, there is something in what Sol says. It
will do you no good to be associated with the King's
men."

"I did what I had to, what was right," Will insisted.

Sol's face was bland as he turned to Will. "It *was*
right — for a Tory."

Will glanced at him. It wasn't the first time Sol
had tried to get him in trouble with their father. Was
he at it again? If so, Will wanted to know for sure.
"Just what does that mean?"

"Only that everyone has a right to his own beliefs.
Yours sound like a Tory's. Perhaps you are one."

For a second Will and his father stared at Sol.
Then Jacob's voice thundered. "Nonsense!"

⌈ Chapter IV ⌋

HIS FATHER'S "nonsense" haunted him all through the summer months and even now he heard the echo of it in the rustling yellow bronze of the oaks that lined Chapel and College Streets and bordered the campus. For the first time in his life the smoky fragrance of autumn failed to excite him. Yale College was different from Master Eaton's school. It was lonelier.

Abe had been in Massachusetts for months. He seldom wrote. His longest letter wasn't a full page, and that had come at the end of June, just after the battle at Breed's Hill. Sol was busier than ever. Will would have laughed aloud at his old plans for being with his brothers but a new self-consciousness restrained him. He was aware at every step that the other students gave him a wide berth on the path.

"Pinto!" A young man in a camlet gown called an order. "Go to my room, middle story of Old College, get my pitcher, fill it at the pump, and wait my return."

Will nodded and quickened his pace, remembering first year men must neither run nor jump in the yard. Zephaniah Swift was a sophomore at Yale College and was entitled to issue commands to freshmen. Well-known as a plain-spoken boy, he took no man's opinion until he had formed his own view. He wasn't one of the more popular members of his class, but one look at his determined face, and Will had liked him. Besides, it was pleasant enough to be spoken to at all, he realized, as he strode along the path in the College Yard.

Throughout the summer he had clutched at a hope that the widely spread story of his aiding a King's man would be as short-lived as it was distorted. Now he knew his hopes were as doomed as the flaming leaves on the maple tree ahead of him, and that they would soon be dead as the brown leaves that already crackled beneath his feet. He heard friendly calls, greetings and laughter, directed above and around him. "Anyone'd think I had the pox," he muttered, as he turned the corner of Chapel toward the faded blue of Old College.

The long narrow building had once been a bright cerulean shade. Now, with the war, no men could be spared to restore its color.

With a flash of pleasure Will saw Solomon coming through the doorway. For a bare half instant their eyes met. Sol looked quickly away. Will's smile froze on his lips. His brother was hurrying along the path to the Commons in step with Ebenezer Daggett. Young Daggett was the youngest son of the college president and Sol daily repeated every word he had with the boy. More than once, Will suspected, he even repeated things he overheard Ebenezer say. Watching his brother now, Will realized Sol had taken to aping the other boy's energetic pace and brisk gravity.

Disgusted, Will strode into the building. It was cooler in the long, paneled hall, but heavily silent and still. In the moment it took his eyes to accustom themselves to the semidarkness, he made out two classmates silhouetted before a posted notice. Only freshmen did not wear the sleek gowns and broad-brimmed hats upperclassmen were entitled to. One boy stood awkwardly, his left hip jutting out to the side. That would be Jonathan Brookley. His peculiar stance made his clubfoot obvious. The other must be Richard Waite. As usual, the two of them were off to themselves, speaking in low voices.

Waite was a pompous-looking young man, richly tailored and with a tendency toward fat. Brookley, equally well dressed, seemed decent enough, though a bit timid for Will's liking. Still, he was the only one in the freshman class who had ever seemed genuinely glad to see Will. Will allowed himself a curt nod and headed for the stairwell. Sol had been quick to tell him the Waites were well-known Tories and Brookley, though uncommitted politically, was suspect by association. "They're good ones to keep away from," his brother had warned. And Will had done just that. Not that he would have if either of the two had really interested him, he had to admit.

He had to pass them to reach the stairs. Briefly he stopped to scan the notice.

The Honorable Fellowship Club
Most Cordially Invites
One and All Gentlemen of Yale College
To Attend
An Extempore Dispute
on
The Moral Right of the Political Independence
of Freeborn Men
This Evening at Nine O'clock,
Chapel Assembly Hall

Will felt the boys' gaze on him as he read.

"Shall you attend the assembly this evening?" Brookley ventured. He spoke in Latin as all the boys within the college halls were supposed to do, but few did, except in the presence of a tutor or professor.

Will smiled at the boy's caution, then shook his head in answer to the question. "I don't think so. I haven't started Tutor Buckminster's assignment in rhetoric and there's not much time left."

Brookley beamed conspiratorily and Richard Waite favored Will with an interested glance. "That's exactly the way we feel," Brookley confided.

They had misunderstood his smile and insinuated their own meaning into his words. Will inched away from them uncomfortably. "I mean —" he began.

Zeph Swift's words cut him short. "Where is that

water pitcher, Pinto?" He came up beside Will, noted Waite, Brookley and the poster. The muscles in his face tightened.

It wasn't hard for Will to see the three of them through Zeph's eyes. Brookley with a grin frozen on his face, and Waite, reaching for Will's arm. They made a pretty picture — a Tory triumvirate.

Oliver Wolcott had come in behind Swift and now he, too, was a witness to the scene. Will looked away from the scorn on the boy's face. Wolcott's father was a general with the Revolutionary forces.

What was there to say? Besides, why should he explain himself to anyone? "I'll get the pitcher," he said. Cursing himself for a fool, Will raced up the stairs.

It was a relief to be home in the large room he shared with Sol. A good room, without distractions, it had just two narrow beds, a chest, a desk and a desk chair, where Will now sat. The floor was bare but spotless, and there were three windows. Best forget the ugly scene with Swift and Wolcott and use the hour of daylight that was left.

He was trying to keep his mind on his book when he heard Sol running up the stairs. Even before his brother thrust open the door Will knew he was angry.

Solomon stood, then banged the door shut behind him.

Reluctantly Will eyed him. "Good news travels fast."

"Very amusing," Sol snapped. He glowered at Will. "Didn't I tell you not to have anything to do with Waite or Brookley? What the devil are you trying to do — alienate yourself from the whole school?"

"Brookley asked me a question and I answered him."

"That's not exactly the way it was put to me." Solomon's voice held the edge of a threat.

"I told you what happened." Will took up his book.

Sol stepped forward and grabbed Will's shoulder. "Don't ignore me."

Will's temper flared. He jumped up. "And don't accuse me of lying! I told you what happened."

For a second they stood, staring at each other furiously. Not a word was spoken, but Will saw his brother's resentment change to bitterness. The silence throbbed with anger. Will had to break it. "Just what *did* you hear?" he demanded.

Sol dropped his hand and turned away. "Daggett told me Oliver Wolcott saw you in a huddle with some Tories making fun of the speech for independence. He said it decently enough — but —"

"But what?"

Sol wouldn't face him. "Nothing, just — well, he was rather cool."

"Why should he be? You didn't do anything."

Sol whirled around. "No, I didn't. But you did. And you're my brother." His face had flushed with anger again.

Will's own fury rushed to meet his brother's. "If Daggett is really your friend, he'll be your friend no matter what I do." He had intended his words to hurt. When he saw they had, he looked swiftly away so as not to lose the satisfaction he felt.

"Daggett's a nice person," Solomon spoke softly now. "I wanted —" he began, stopped, then, "Oh, Will, aren't we different enough from the others? I've tried so hard. And now —"

Will hadn't counted on the plea in his brother's voice. It spoiled his own triumph. Annoyed, he spoke gruffly. "Different because we're Jews and no one will let us forget it? What kind of independence is this all about? Independence from a King you were never loyal to? Independence for yourself or for Daggett?" Will laughed bitterly.

"Independence for my country," Sol answered steadily.

"*Your* country? *Your* country that denies citizenship to a man because he's a Jew? *Your* country that buys and sells Africans? An Englishman's country, that's what this war's about. For Englishmen who love their freedom so dearly they want to keep it to themselves. Rot."

Silence hung between them for long seconds.

"Then you won't come to the assembly tonight?" Solomon's voice was resigned. His eyes seemed to search for help somewhere, anywhere but from the brother who denied it.

Will saw Solomon's helplessness. Now he understood all Sol's warnings against Waite and Brookley, against Mr. Eaton, in favor of the "right" associations. These warnings had been given, not out of concern for Will, but out of fear for himself. Will knew and was hurt. But he felt pity for Sol. "Yes, I will go," he said.

[Chapter V]

EVEN BEFORE they entered the chapel Will felt
the emotion that throbbed from within. Approv-
ing shouts, hand-clapping and whistles echoed in the
hall. The strong scent of excitement itched up inside his nose and he quickened his step hurrying
after Solomon and Ebenezer Daggett. A roar of huz-
zahs resounded as Sol reached for the doorknob. Politely Solomon signaled Daggett ahead of him and
motioned Will to hurry.

They stepped into the great oak-beamed room. A
young man stood on the middle rostrum, the largest
of three burnished wood pulpits. He waved his arms
to emphasize words he shouted above enthusiastic
comments made freely by students, tutors, and the
few townspeople who thronged the hall.

Enormous vitality churned through the audience
like a whirlpool. For a second Will struggled against
its force, tried to get his bearings and find three seats.

He saw two together on the aisle near the door where they stood. Daggett pointed out another one in the first row, directly in front of the speaker. Will nodded and headed for it.

He settled himself into his chair and tried to isolate the speaker's words from the confusion that hummed through the hall. Phrase by phrase he began to catch the familiar arguments. Now the speaker quoted Isaac Barre's famous attack on the British Parliament. "The colonists? . . . children planted by your care?" The words had been repeated so often the audience caught them up and chanted along with the orator. "No!" they roared in unison. "Your oppression planted them in America,". . .

"They were nourished by your indulgence?"

"They grew by your neglect." The young speaker's face grew red at the pulsating heady sounds. "The words of a member of the King's Parliament," he shouted, "and what did he call us?" The question crescendoed exultantly.

"Sons of Liberty!" the crowd roared back.

Will smiled to himself. This was fun. Above the roaring and shouting, the heat of the cause bound them all together. He settled back to enjoy more.

The second speaker retold the history of the King's soldiers in the colonies, how the hard-working colonists were forced to lodge and feed them. Gradually he changed the mood in the hall. He roused the audience to fury with stories of atrocities committed by the hated redcoats. Good fellowship turned to anger — restless, black, ugly.

And suddenly Will could hear the breaking china, Elias Eaton's moans, Thomas Crull's ignorant cussing. His stomach sickened, his body grew tense and he stiffened in his chair. Memory of a dank cellar sent a cold tremor of fear through him. But these are not drunken bullies, he reassured himself, they're gentlemen of Yale College.

"Still the King kept soldiers in the colonies," the speaker went on.

I'll wager none of the colonists objected to those soldiers' helping them fight the Indians. Will's anger brought him to his feet. He opened his mouth to speak, suddenly remembered the plea on Solomon's face, and stood speechless, unable to sit down.

"You disagree, sir? Mr. Pinto, I believe?" The boy on the rostrum looked directly at Will. The quick silence was louder than any noise Will had heard all evening. Every face in the room turned on him. Waiting, judging faces.

"Well?" the speaker demanded. His face, too, impatient now.

"I —" Will began. He looked at all those faces and knew he could see only one, one behind him and probably too frightened to look at him. He lowered his head. "Nn–no. Ex–excuse me, please," he mumbled and stepped over the legs that separated him from escape.

Head still down, he hurried along the aisle to the door, racing to keep ahead of the embarrassment, the horror, of what he had done. Passing Sol, his step faltered and his eyes slid to his brother's face.

Solomon sat motionless and white as chalk. His lips did not move, but a sound twisted through them. "Damn you."

Will jerked himself forward and fled in horror of what he had done, of his brother's face.

Outside he did not follow the path to College Street and the town. He went in the other direction, circling behind the Chapel and making a wide detour around the College Commons. The Yard was deserted now, still, and nearly dark. It was lighted only faintly by a moon that slid in and out behind heavy clouds, causing leafy shadows to change shape swiftly, disappear into blackness and suddenly reappear ahead, to the side, or behind him.

The rhythm of horses' hooves on the cobblestone street sent him faster. As they came closer he melted into the kindness of a clump of evergreens. The smell of pine was rich, sweet, and soothing. He felt the rising wind wash over his face and saw the silver undersides of pine needles. Then, hardly knowing where his feet were taking him, he raced, forgetting or no longer caring about decorum and rules.

Quickly he came to the far side of the Yard. He mustn't go too close to the fence and town. A dense shape loomed on his right, a thicket of vines, shrubs, and several young elms.

He singled out a narrow opening and bent low, feeling his way, fairly crawling through the tunnel-like path toward the small space at the thicket's center. Then, the boy flung himself down.

Soft, moist, and warm beneath him, the earth comforted him. The first soft drops of rain sounded on the leaves above. Sheltered by the foliage, his body rested. But his mind raced. He had gone to the meeting to please Solomon. Now he had disgraced him. Once he had stood up in obvious disagreement, he should have had the courage to speak. In front of the whole College he had appeared a coward as well as a Tory. Sol had been eager, even anxious to forgive him before, but now —

With a jerk Will sat up, made a fist and pounded it against the earth. If Solomon weren't such a fool he'd know it's my shame, not his. Besides, I have a right to my opinions. I don't give a fig for their stupid war and they might as well know it.

Abruptly he stood upright and strode through the thicket into a misty rain. When he reached the main gate he was still scowling.

He felt the cold rain pricks, heavier now, as he crossed Chapel Street and turned into Elm. Little rivulets of water ran among the cobblestones, seeped up through his thick soles, dampening his socks.

One hanging lantern still glowed. It swayed slightly beneath a sign that read Old Swan's Inn, well-known meeting place for King's men. That's all I'd need now — to be seen in there. Will smiled to himself as he hurried by the tavern light.

Not too much further home, less than a mile. Across Drugby Lane, turn left. For a few minutes the click of his wooden heels resounded in the street. He hoped his father would be asleep by the time he reached the house, and walked slowly now to insure his hope. Behind him a carriage clattered around a corner, heading toward him. Without looking back, Will stepped aside and kept walking.

The coach rushed past him, then stopped quickly. It was black and handsome and the light of the lamp on its side set its bronze ornaments gleaming. Jonathan Brookley leaned out of the window. "May I offer you a ride, Mr. Pinto?"

Will hesitated. He was getting wetter and colder each minute. He shook his head. "No, thanks, I haven't much more to go."

Brookley waved his hand and drew back inside. In another moment he had the door open and was lowering himself awkwardly into the street. Will could see his face in the lamplight. The boy's smile flickered embarrassment. "Look, I don't like to press you, Will, but my sister's with me and she says this isn't a fit night for anyone to walk."

It was the second plea in one night he should have resisted and did not, Will thought, as he sank back into the cushions of the Brookleys' carriage. Its unexpected comfort sent a shiver through him. He wiped his hand across his face and was surprised to find himself sopping wet. He shook his hand dry.

"Watch you don't drown us all," Elizabeth Brookley said.

He could barely make out the girl's features, but even in the darkness her smile warmed him.

"Why don't you stop at our house for something hot? We live just around the turn," Jonathan said.

He offered an answer to Will's weakening objection before the boy could utter it. "I'll take you home soon as you're dry."

It was a fine house covered with white oak clapboards and solidly built in the strong simple lines of the Georgian style. The gambrel roof was topped with several broad chimneys and broken by dormer windows.

They entered a large doorway. In the center hall, just to Will's left, was a stairway gracefully designed and handsomely carved. Elizabeth led them into a drawing room; its fireplace was well proportioned and there was a simple mantel above the crackling fire.

Will headed toward it. He held his hands out and stood while the flames' heat licked him dry. Now he turned to warm his back and saw the girl watching him.

She was about his age and height, with thin, plain features. Only her eyes held a reminder of her smile. Barely green, they were centered, circled and flecked by the soft bronze color of her hair.

He saw the tea tray. There was a gleaming silver pot, a matching sugar and creamer, but just two cups and only a few sweet cakes. Suddenly Will was ravenous.

The girl seemed to read his mind. Within minutes she was out of the room and back carrying a tray filled with thick slices of freshly baked bread spread to the corners with bright yellow butter, a pot of strawberry-rich jam, and another teacup.

Will ate hungrily, relishing every bite, nodding

occasionally to questions so phrased a man busily eating need only nod. It was pleasant and easy to listen to her direct tones and Jonathan's companionable response.

Just as he swallowed the last crumb, Will found himself earnestly discussing Tutor Kent's assignment with Jonathan. While the boys talked Elizabeth said little. Her presence added zest to their conversation and time raced, gathering momentum from ease, laughter and honest warmth.

The clock on the mantel chimed twelve times. Will jumped up. Probably, he thought, I've overstayed my welcome.

Fifteen minutes later when Jonathan Brookley slowed the coach to a quiet stop not quite in front of the Pintos' house, Will knew the boy shared his sister's intuitiveness.

It was hard to thank someone for an inborn trait. "Good night, Brookley."

The boy smiled. Will did not need to say more.

[Chapter VI]

LATE THE NEXT MORNING he woke, up vaguely uneasy. One glance at Sol's face, tightly asleep, reminded him of the reason. Will dressed quickly, slipped out of the house before anyone else was awake, and headed toward the center of town.

Nearly everyone came to the Green at some time during training day. The custom had begun years ago with the organization and training of the militia and had grown into a monthly gathering of the whole town. Now it was a sort of mart where young people paraded their gayest clothes and farmers brought their wives and children in carts stuffed with squealing pigs, great round cheeses, fresh-picked vegetables, and yellow-billed ducks. Will liked the fall training days best when, like today, new cider spiced the fragrance of fresh-cut hay and warm cattle smells. There were fruit tarts to buy and miles of bright winter yarn and apples that cracked hard and tart in the mouth. The air was crisp and set blood racing. Men and boys competed for prizes in shooting, wrestling and running. They called out wagers and livened them with hearty jokes.

A race was just beginning. "Here, lad," a man in shirt sleeves and a three-cornered hat called to him. "Want to try for the prize?"

There were six in the line and he could see the man needed more contestants. He'd seen the bazaar and the games, and there was no reason to stay. But he did want to talk to Jonathan Brookley, and if Elizabeth — no, it was Jonathan he wanted to see, and then, he should be here soon. Till then he might as well race. "Why not?" He stepped up to the man.

"Why not, indeed? That's the spirit. Anyone else for a try?" Still calling, the starter hustled Will into place, pointed out the course, and beaming, patted the boy's back. "Runners' contest, lads," he shouted with new vigor. "A whole dollar for the winner." The man's face glistened from his effort.

Will smiled. No one trusted the new paper money. But the race would work off some of his restlessness.

The starter re-lined the contestants, straightened the marking ribbon and managed to herd two more boys out of the gathering crowd. "A hundred rods across the field," he explained again. Will didn't bother listening. He turned and scanned the onlookers, forcing himself to do it casually. Then in spite of himself his heart quickened.

The crowd parted as Elizabeth slipped into the front row. Her brother and Richard Waite stepped forward to flank her. They stood like guards protecting her from the disapproving townspeople. Instinctively, the villagers left a wide space around the three of them.

If Elizabeth noticed, she didn't let it show. She stood easily, holding her bonnet by its strings. Uncovered, her tawny hair fell on her shoulders, trapping the sun's gold about her face.

Suddenly Will wanted to win. Unexplicable excitement itched inside him. Now he looked eagerly toward the post he must race for, touch, and then return from. Carefully he judged the distance as he placed his left foot directly on the starting line. His right foot behind him, he crouched low for a quick start. For the first time he observed his competitors. Big muscular farm lads, for the most part. Just a few Yale men. He recognized Wolcott, Jr., and, next to him, his classmate, Noah Webster, a slim, vigorous boy. Tall, fine, fair-skinned lads, the right sort to attract the attention of Miss Elizabeth Brookley. Will grinned. Should he beat them, those clear sea eyes would be his — if just for a moment.

"On your mark, get set to be ready —" Will's heart pounded to the sound of the words. He thrust his head forward. "Get ready —" An eternity of waiting. "Go!"

He shot forward, not daring to waste a second of energy to glance to either side of him. The wind stung past his face. He heard the roar of the crowd and felt more than saw the boy who kept pace abreast of him. On the other side a red-shirted figure flashed by. Wolcott. Will plunged on into air suddenly heavy and hard to penetrate. A stab of pain cut into his side and for a second it was hard to breathe. He forced himself on. Harder. Faster. Still faster and he was running alone. No one beside him and only Wolcott ahead. For a fleeting instant an unreasoning desire to win gripped him. Nothing else mattered. Not the prize. Not Elizabeth Brookley.

The post was just ahead. He reached out, grabbed it, and swung himself around it. He thrust himself forward now, blind to everything. A loose stone slipped under his shoe, sent him stumbling forward. Sheer willpower held his balance and Will hurled himself on in a last burst of effort that sent him beyond Wolcott and across the finish line, breathless, triumphant.

His chest heaved and his pulse throbbed. Then he saw Elizabeth. He could only smile and nod as the man handed him the paper dollar and voices called out their congratulations. Still barely able to catch his breath, he cut across the Green and proudly, in full view of the villagers, stepped up to face Elizabeth Brookley.

"Good race, Will." Jonathan smiled.

"You ran as though the devil was after you," Elizabeth laughed.

Amazed, Will stared at her. In truth that was just the way he felt.

Jonathan laughed. "Good thing Liz wasn't born fifty years ago, or she'd have been hanged for a mind-reading witch by now."

Will was sure the girl had no idea what happened to her face when she smiled as she now did.

"They'd have had me to answer to," Waite declared with such pomposity Will almost laughed.

Liz's eyes, too, filled with mirth. "I could use you at the schoolhouse, Richard. Sometimes I have the feeling Master Eaton's students would like to hang me."

"Then you're really helping the old man?" Waite's alarm was faintly disapproving.

She nodded. "He needs help. Ever since that awful night."

Waite's lower lip thrust forward as a petulant child's. Plainly he didn't care to have her mingling with the farm lads and shopkeepers' sons in the classroom.

"He is your cousin, Richard." Jonathan was making it seem as though Elizabeth's concern was for Waite's family.

"He's only a third cousin," Waite mumbled, though obviously he had been mollified.

The girl would have none of it. "I'm helping him because he needs me. And because I despise bullies. Disloyal ones especially," she declared hotly.

"Ssh," her brother warned. He glanced at the throng that milled about.

"I will not hush." With a swift movement of her head, Elizabeth tossed her hair back on her shoulder and raised her voice. She seemed willing to state her opinion to anyone who cared to listen. "This rebellion is just an excuse for lawbreakers. And for boys who want to play soldier." Her eyes flashed. "Why can't they talk out their grievances like reasonable men?"

If Waite hadn't agreed with such quick admiration, Will might have concurred. As it was, his own anger rose. His brother wasn't "playing soldier," and whether she knew it or not, his father *was* a reasonable man.

"In any case, you ran a fine race, Will." Jonathan's discomfort forced a change of subject. "Yes," Liz said quickly, "really wonderful to watch." Her eyes sparkled in admiration.

"No doubt running's in the blood." Richard Waite seemed bent on drawing the girl's attention from the other boy. "I expect," he said to Will, "your father fled as quickly from the Catholics."

"With no more haste than yours left England," Will snapped. "And it was my grandfather who escaped the Spanish Inquisition."

Waite's barely visible eyebrows rose. "Our family's land grant was a token of esteem from King Charles, hardly given to rid the country of my people."

Will's temper flared. He groped for a retort, but Elizabeth's response was instant. Laughing, she replied, "I thought the children of Abraham were sent forth by a more divine authority than Charles."

Will nearly choked with delight as Richard's face flushed pink.

But Elizabeth couldn't enjoy someone else's discomfort. She turned her smile on Waite. "Is there something else you wanted to see, Richard, or shall we start home?"

It was easy to see the boy was dazed by that smile. "Your choice, Elizabeth."

Jonathan nodded. "Coming, Will?"

Will glanced at the girl. She had linked her arm through Waite's. So that was the way it was. "No, I think I'll stay."

Only after they left did Will realize he was alone in the wide gap the crowd left around them. Waite, the Brookleys, and Will Pinto had stood isolated in the center of New Haven Green.

Sol was standing at the shop door waiting for him. "Father wants to see you at once," he said rigidly.

"I take it you've already seen him."

"Of course." Sol was stiff with righteousness.

Will didn't answer. He pushed past him and into the shop.

The light was dim, but his father's eyes burned fiercely. "I will not accept flagrant disobedience from a member of my household." Jacob Pinto's heavy eyebrows massed together in a dark line of wrath. Abigail, moving softly behind the counter, dusting the pin boxes on the shelf, was a barely noticed shadow. Her pale calm pointed up her husband's fury. "Not only have you embarrassed your brother at the College, now you have made a display of your new associations on the Green. Traitors! That's what they are! And that's what you'll be called."

"The British army won't call them traitors when

your rebellion is finally put down, Jacob." Abigail's tone was mild, but she shocked father and son into speechlessness. Without change of motion or manner she continued, "And it shall be put down. Thirteen small colonies have no chance against Britain. Then your 'traitors' will be heroes." She folded her dusting cloth into the pocket of her apron and took up her broom.

Unlike the expression on his face, Jacob's voice was gentle. "I understand your concern, but you know well it is basically wrong to expect self-respecting men to work for a distant king first and themselves afterwards."

What devil possessed Will to defy his father? "Then this War for Independence is really a War for Profit?" He knew he was begging for a beating, but lately every word of Jacob's became an affront. Will repeatedly challenged the old man to prove him wrong. Bewildered, ashamed, Will stared at the wide floorboards, waiting.

Even the sharp whisk of Abigail's broom had stopped. Will hoped the blow would come soon. But Jacob knew words that had more power than a blow. "The Lord delivered us from the Egyptian pharaoh. Isn't it possible He means to save us from another tyrant? Didn't Spain crumble under a decadent monarch?"

"I thought the British fleet smashed the Spanish Armada." Will couldn't give in.

"Ha! You know the British navy wasn't a match for Spain's ships. Oh, the English did some damage, but after a few days they were exhausted. And the Armada planned another attack, but they ran into one storm after another. It was those storms finished what England had begun. Have any of your professors been able to explain those unseasonable storms?"

"Then we need not fight. God will destroy our enemies."

Abigail gasped at Will's blasphemy.

But Jacob remained maddeningly calm. "Is it God or your father you mock, William? Do not think me such a fool I do not know God will help us when He sees we have the courage to stand and face our enemy."

"Then you think I lack that courage?"

"I think you lack conviction. It will come, in time." Jacob took the large black ledger from the shelf and placed it on the worn counter top he often used as desk. He picked up his quill and began to turn the pages of his accounts. "Meanwhile, stay out of trouble."

"You mean I can't see Brookley or Waite?" Or Elizabeth, he added silently.

"Exactly."

The subject was closed. Angrily, Will snatched up his cap and started for the door. Where could he go? Home? Sol would be there, with his friends. Back to the Green? He'd hardly be welcome there. Besides, the contests were probably over. The College? He had a long book list he hadn't bothered with. The boy kicked aimlessly at a keg in the aisle. He wasn't in the mood for reading.

His father seemed to read his thoughts. "Attend to your studies, Will, and await your brother Abraham's return." Jacob looked up from his work and, for the first time that day, smiled.

Will felt his breath catch in his throat. "Abe?" Was Abe really coming home?

As though he were giving his son a gift, Jacob said, "Abraham's been allowed a short furlough. He doesn't know exactly when, but it will be sometime soon. Probably early December."

Suddenly everything was different. Abe was coming home! The words beat wildly through him. Who needs Brookley when Abe is coming? He laughed aloud and grabbed for the door. He'd race through those books as fast as Dr. Prescott to Concord. Nothing must keep him from spending time with Abe.

[Chapter VII]

EACH DAY darkness came earlier and brought Abraham nearer home. And then there was just one more night! Abe would be home tomorrow! Will pulled his thin coat closer about him and turned up its collar against the cold. He felt the letter of commendation crinkle against his side and he smiled. He had done well this fall term. Now with Abe home he could slide through the next fortnight. And the letter, with all its fine compliments, especially the ones on penmanship, would please Abe. It might even tickle his funnybone. Abe's laugh could chase the gloom from the dourest day — or from the loneliest boy.

Will tucked his fists inside his sleeves and sucked in his stomach. Food was in short supply. Months ago Governor Trumbull had requested voluntary restrictions and his father ordered Abigail to ration even more strictly now. They would feast when Abe came home. Just the thought of the warm spicy kitchen smells these past few days set Will's mouth watering and his feet scurrying.

In the quickening dimness he saw a cloaked figure bobbing grotesquely toward him. Guilty, a bit ashamed, he slipped around a corner into a shopway and waited. He had no wish to meet Jonathan Brookley tonight. Nothing must spoil the anticipation of his brother's homecoming. Jonathan had been puzzled by his sudden coolness, Will knew. Though the boy had asked him nothing, had made no demands on him, it was hard to face him. It was especially hard now that people were boycotting the Brookleys' granary. Jonathan's clothes were less fashionable and there was talk his roan was up for sale. Will scowled. It isn't my fault his father refused to sell their wheat at the Army's price, he thought angrily. Why doesn't he smuggle it out to the British as the Waites do? While he asked himself, he had already guessed the answer. If Master Brookley were anything like Jonathan or Elizabeth, he was far too honest for that. They'd probably rather starve. The thought of Elizabeth's being hungry sent a wave of nausea through his belly and up, choking, into his throat. Stupid, righteous gentiles! Savagely he kicked at a cobblestone. Nonsense! Richard Waite would never let her starve. Not the way he had looked at her. Somewhat comforted, Will still could not manage to quell the nagging suspicion that Elizabeth would never ask for anything. Curse this war.

From what Abraham said in his letters, there

hadn't been a battle since June. Through summer and fall General Washington had the troops spread out around Boston waiting for the surrounded red-coats to attack or evacuate. Meanwhile the rebels did little but train and stand guard. Once or twice, Abe wrote, they'd exchanged a few shots with the British sentries and occasionally fired on guard boats. These were just skirmishes. Still, Johnny Russell came home without a foot and Mistress Wiggim knew the child she carried was an orphan. But nothing of military importance occurred.

It would, though, soon. And Abe would be back there when it did. His enlistment term ended December 10, so he had signed up again. Why? Will wondered at that and wondered too at the deep pride he felt in his soldier brother.

And now there was only one more night. Then Abe would be home.

Abraham arrived with the sun. Snow had cleansed the town, softened the bare angles of the houses. A rare winter brightness transformed New Haven.

Will was first to hear muted hooves. He raced to the door, and the others followed.

Bronze, tall, broader and heavier than Will remembered, glowing with a new manhood but beaming an old smile, Abe strode through the unmarked snow. The family stood on the stoop, somehow sensing together the rightness that Abraham's feet cut the first welcome into the white.

And then Abe was upon them, his great arms

about them all, in a reunion that boomed joy to the sky.

Will watched Abe's white teeth bite into thick slices of gravy-rich meat, pudding heavy with long-saved sage and sweet with thyme, cranberries strained through silver mesh to a sauce, and new-caught fish, bubbling brown and butter-fat.

He ate with voracious pleasure. Abigail's usually colorless face went pink with pride when Abe reached for a third apple tart.

But Jacob and Sol were hungry for news of the war. Jacob hadn't touched the food on his plate. Fork in hand, he leaned toward his eldest son. Sol's eyes too were intent on Abe's face as he talked.

"We're short of everything — food, powder, decent shelter — but the cold's the worst of it. A man's likely to cut another's throat for a few sticks of wood. We're desperate for warm clothes, blankets and fuel. Most of the men can't see why they're not allowed to return home when all they've done for months is wait for an attack." Abe shook his head. "There's more deserters than you'd believe.

"As it is, we're not strong enough to attack them, and every day that we don't is a victory for the redcoats. New York's the place for their offensive and they know it, but Gage won't abandon the Tories in Boston. Why should he? All he has to do is wait for winter to dissolve our forces."

Jacob's fist sounded resolutely on the table. "We've got to get you more supplies."

Abe nodded. "Connecticut and Rhode Island enlistments end in a few days, and by the end of the month all New England terms expire."

"You re-enlisted," Sol said.

"Aye. Those of us who did got furloughs to go home for our winter clothes. But many refused to sign up. One company, to a man, marched off." Abe glanced at his father, whose face was grim. "It's a sorry business."

"But it must be done," Jacob said.

"It must," Abe agreed. He went on, but Will was far too excited to listen.

It was Abe's presence and the sound of his voice that stirred Will's pleasure. And the feel of the fine linen napkin, the taste of sugar were doubly sweet because they had almost been forgotten, as had the smells of a heavily laden table. With the sight of them all, their faces pleasure-bright — all of it — Will had never felt so full.

Snatches of conversation struck him — "Maybe General Washington will force the British out of Boston . . . perhaps the General Assembly will supply powder and food . . . confiscate loyalist property."

While Abigail cleared away the dishes, Abe pushed back from the table. His tone changed. It was rich with affection and merriment as he pinched Abigail's cheek, "I'm going to bring you the biggest, fattest, finest turkey in Connecticut. Big enough to last a week." He looked down at his belly, patted it and corrected himself, "Well, two days, anyway." Abi-

gail's laughter was ready as their own, spilled out because Abe always made them laugh. And because, at
last, he was home. Whole. Safe.

"Who'll hunt with me?" He looked at Sol and
Will.

Will jerked forward in his chair. "I —" he began
but Sol jumped up, ran across the room, grabbed his
books and called, "School! I almost forgot! We're
late already. Hurry, Will!"

Blast school, Will thought, when I can be hunting
with Abe. Reluctantly the boy rose. The heavy door
opened and banged closed behind Solomon. Jacob
stood slowly. "I must go to my work also. And you to
yours, William."

Their father turned. Abigail held his coat out for
him.

"Your books, boy. Mustn't forget them," Abe
teased. "I'll walk along with you." With a long, easy
reach he picked up two heavy volumes, made a low,
ceremonious bow, then grinning, looked up at Will
and winked.

"Let's see if it's still there." Abe pointed his finger, counting. Elm, maple, birch, elm again to the
left. "Yup. There she is — Mother Nature's Aid to
the Wayward Student." He laughed, scooped Will's
books from his hand and thrust them into a snug
knothole. He patted the tree's trunk. "She's a faith-
ful old guardian. Kept a remarkable number of distinguished gentlemen safe for me — Masters Tully,
Virgil, Cicero. Once housed an ancient Greek for a
fortnight. Remember that old stag I brought home?"

Will grinned. "How could I forget? If he was as tough to track as he was to chew —" Will rubbed his jaws reminiscently.

"Tough? I tracked him five days while Aristotle waited. Then I forgot where I had put the old windbag." Abe chuckled. "It was a real Greek tragedy 'til I remembered."

The boys smiled widely at each other. They ducked in and out among the trees, heading deeper into the woods. Rifles were slung over their shoulders, and their feet crunched over the snow in a crackling military rhythm. Wind sang against their faces and Will breathed in the excitement of the clean cold air. Strength and freedom soared inside him.

They walked for miles, deep into the woods until the sun was directly overhead. Abe headed for a roost he had often hunted. The closer they came, the more silent they must be. Will walked behind his brother, watching carefully to put his foot down at the exact moment Abe did. The crack of a twig could make a flock fade ghostlike into the woods.

An occasional crow cawed, and once they heard the short, high bark of a she fox. The stillness of the winter wood made breathing loud. Cold turned it to a smoke signal.

Will's fingers were cold. His gun grew heavy and his legs began to ache. Without Abe's determination he knew he would turn back. Half an hour, three quarters, and at last he saw the unmistakable windrows of scratchings. Needles of excitement pricked at his neck. He poked Abe's back with his gun butt. Without turning, Abe nodded, and the younger boy's chest pounded in that shared fear-thrill of hunters at first sight of hunted. Will's body tensed. He could hear his own life-beat, and was somehow sure his brother pulsed in exact rhythm.

Abe held up his hand. Will stopped behind him. There was the bareness of trees, the gray of space between, the white of snow, and everywhere silence. Without a word between them they took each step, each second, each breath together.

Now, in sight of the roost, the wait began. Shadows darkened but instinct blotted time and hunger while they listened. It came. The sound of scratchings, then gobbling. The boys' eyes locked in triumph, and then fastened on the roost high in the trees. A brush of wings, and two shots sounded as one.

They had aimed at the same bird. That, too, was in keeping with the day and their triumph.

Abe reached down, took the turkey by its feet, and slung it over his shoulder. He pretended to stagger under its weight and Will laughed aloud. Perhaps it wasn't the biggest, fattest bird in Connecticut, but it was an embarrassment to no man.

Whistling, singing, yelling back and forth like children just let out of school, they took the long way home around the quickly darkening woods, across the meadows.

As they came closer to town, the path widened. Beyond the bend it would became a road. Evening came fast this time of year but Will hoped there would still be people abroad in the village. It was a proud thing to walk beside Abraham.

They reached the turn. Will felt a second's disappointment. One lone figure walked on Elm Street. Then his eyes set his heart racing. Elizabeth. He slowed his step, hoping that would slow his pulse. He could feel Abe's quick glance and he blushed, knowing his brother's sharp perception. A few more seconds and they would pass her, close enough to touch.

Elizabeth hurried. She carried a basket over her arm and the hood of her gray cloak covered her hair. She walked quickly, purposefully.

He knew he must wait for her to speak and he was glad of it. He hardly trusted his voice these days. Sometimes it came out deep as Abe's, more often it was a boyish squeak. He tried to clear his throat silently.

Elizabeth's warm smile and "Hello, Will" startled him. He felt himself flush furiously. Almost before he could answer she hurried by.

He turned and watched, his greeting following her. She half faced him again, waving briefly.

He stood rooted till she was out of sight. Abe's voice surprised him into movement. "So Little Will has a girl," his brother teased. He felt Abe's arm on his shoulder. "And a fine-looking young lady she is." Abe's face shone warm for Will's pleasure.

The boy's discomfort vanished. "Her name's Elizabeth." He surprised himself at the confidence.

"A good strong name," Abe noted.

Warmed, Will heard his own words tumble out everything he knew about the girl. When he repeated what she had told Waite on the Green, Abe howled with delight.

"Still, Richard Waite seems to have some claim on her," Will said.

"He would be a sensible choice for a Brookley," Abe said solemnly and his eyes twinkled. "But women aren't always sensible."

"Come on," Will yelled. "Race you the rest of the way home."

Chapter VIII

WILL BURST into the kitchen, breathless and laughing, in time to see Abe fall into a chair. Abe put a warning finger to his lips. "Ssh. Father has a visitor."

"Will? Is Abraham with you?" Jacob called from the company room.

"Yes, sir."

"Bring him in here, boy."

Abe rose and Will followed. He recognized Mr. Roger Sherman, treasurer of Yale College and a member of the Connecticut Senate, a distinguished gentleman, well respected throughout the colony. He had wide-set, clear eyes, a strong nose, and a generous mouth. Responsibility etched every line on his face. Both he and Jacob rose as the boys entered the room.

"I would like you to meet my son Abraham, sir." There was magnificence in the simple words. For the first time Will saw his father as other men did. The eyes burned with fierce pride in a face so strong, so controlled it masked the ferment that lay beneath. It was this same strength that had taken him from his own father's house in Stratford to New Haven, had allowed him to marry a Christian woman and year after year refuse the comfort of both churches. And it was this strength too that remained unfaltering when he sent his first-born son to war. Was this inheritance entailed? Did it belong only to the eldest son? Will, wondering, ached.

Now Jacob smiled to include Will. "And my son William, sir."

Mr. Sherman nodded and smiled but it was Abe's eyes he sought.

"I'm sorry the other gentlemen left before you arrived. We'd been discussing the danger of King's men in our midst and whether we should petition the Council of Safety to warn the Tories out of New Haven. Something must be done. What do you think?"

Abe glanced at Jacob, who waited, as did Will and Roger Sherman.

Will held his breath. Tell them, Abe, he begged silently. Tell them it's wrong. He saw the flush that darkened his brother's face. Will gripped his lip with his teeth. Abe was pondering too long, looking again to their father. Jacob's eyes refused an answer.

He's giving you a chance, Abe. Tell them about Eaton. Elizabeth, too. Say it's unfair, Will almost cried out. They'll listen to you.

Abe's brows formed a black line of concentration. Again his eyes sought their father's. Finally his face eased into a smile. Will turned from it.

"Learning to fight doesn't leave much time for thinking, sir. That's best left to men like you and my father." Now he laughed fully. "Even Will here's always had more inclination to philosophy than I. I'd venture he has an opinion."

Will grabbed the opportunity.

"Yes, sir, I do. I believe you risk destroying innocent people." His voice shrilled urgently till it was a squeak so childish the man laughed.

"Time will give him wisdom and voice to speak," Jacob said quickly.

Will reddened.

"Did you decide there should be such a petition?" Abe asked.

"Not yet, but we must be free from fear of disloyal neighbors," Master Sherman answered. "I don't see any alternative."

"But we mustn't fear without reasonable cause," Jacob cautioned.

Is he placating me, Will wondered. Is he showing me how reasonable their war is? Or is he trying to force me to think his way?

"We must," Jacob continued, "be careful not to lose sight of our cause. Each man must have the freedom to choose his side. Our hardest job will be to determine the honesty of each decision."

"And sentiment cannot sway what we determine."

Roger Sherman's statement waited for Jacob's affirmation.

Slowly, almost sadly, Jacob caught Abe's eye and together they nodded agreement.

Once more the invisible circle closed, leaving Will outside.

He mumbled "good night," and excused himself. Abigail was waiting outside the door.

"Will, your supper," she whispered.

Will followed her into the kitchen and mechanically ate the hot food she served him. Her gentleness annoyed him. He pushed back his chair and mumbled another "good night."

Fear thumped at his chest as he climbed the stairs to his room. How could he align himself with men who might force Elizabeth from her home? He longed to believe, as he knew Abraham and Jacob did, that the patriots' cause superseded any one person. But how could Jacob honestly support such an idea — he who often spoke with bitterness of the Inquisition, of heads that rolled in the name of a cause?

Jacob's own father, Will's grandfather, Abraham Pinto, had been forced to leave Spain by a Church convinced every non-Catholic was a threat to its survival. He fled to Portugal, but the persecution spread there. Any perils in the New World seemed preferable, so he came to the colonies, bringing with him memories that horrified Jacob and even his sons. Children orphaned by an "iron maiden" — the apparatus of execution shaped into the figure of a woman and lined with spikes that closed at the touch of a spring and then opened above a yawning pit into which the mangled remains dropped — mothers who drowned their babies rather than let them know such cruelty and, more terrifying than all else, priests who believed God favored their work, who could point out their triumphs until even the most enlightened, including Abraham Pinto, began to wonder if there were not just one road to God's heart.

Wasn't persecution in the name of God or country still persecution? Wasn't any cause wrong if it was responsible for one family's flight, one death? He fell into bed exhausted, his mind whirling with questions he couldn't answer.

The house was so still he could hear Sol breathing in the bed beside him. Moonlight slipped ghostlike through the windowpane. A soft rustle of leaves whispered outside. Will lay motionless, every nerve in his body alert. A sixth sense warned him against sleep. He fought against the warning, burying his head in the pillow turning its ends up over his ears to shut out sounds he kept expecting to hear.

Silence stifled time. Will felt as though he were suspended in a vacuum. Waiting. When the shout finally came it was a relief.

"Fire!"

He slipped out of bed. Every man would be needed. Still, this couldn't be the reason for his wakefulness. How many times had he had to be roused to join a water line? Why was tonight different? Whatever reason, he was glad for an excuse to be up and moving.

Outside his window the calls for help multiplied. "Sol, wake up." He shook his brother. "Fire! Come on."

Sol rolled over, but his eyes were closed. Will glanced outside. The sky showed no signs of a blaze. "Wake up," he hissed again. No need yet to wake the others. There'd be enough young men without bothering his father, and Abe deserved the rest. He buckled his shoes, and once more bent over Solomon. "You coming?"

"Hm. Yeh, coming." His eyelids fluttered.

"Well, hurry. I'm going." He started for the door. "You sure you're awake?"

No answer.

The devil with him. Noiselessly he let himself out of the bedroom. Now, down the stairs, through the kitchen, and outside.

The air was warmer than it had been all day, and there was no wind to fan the fire. He still couldn't see any flame, but he heard the running feet and the calls. "The church. Bring pails." He headed toward the sounds. A man ran past him.

"Is it the church?" Will called.

"The school, I heard," the man answered, and for a second Will stood. Then suddenly he was running. Master Eaton. Had they done it to him again? The faster he ran the faster his thoughts came. Of course. Chosen a windless night. Mustn't threaten their own. But destroy an old man. Burn his books.

He ran. He saw the sky grow light with flame. Fury burned within him. He blundered on into the smells and sounds, rushing by groups of men and boys moving slowly as he had at first. "Hurry," he shouted angrily. Why hadn't he forced Sol out?

Each second made the light brighter, louder. He could hear the crowd, the calls for water, more men, buckets, and then he turned the corner and saw vicious orange tongues licking hungrily at the frame building — Master Eaton's schoolhouse.

Flames lighted the line of sweating, grunting men, the swarm of hurrying, excited boys, and clucking flocks of night-capped goodwives. Beyond them houses, the College tower, church steeple stood indifferent in their undisturbed safety. Bells clanged, horses whinnied fearfully, timbers crashed. Above all the commotion came Elias Eaton's unbelieving words, "My books, my years of books." The keening voice drew Will's eyes to the bent figure. Will pushed and jostled his way through the crowd.

"Hey, teacher's pet. If it ain't Wee Willie." Thomas Crull's sneer set a new blaze in Will. Without plan his fists were ready, raised, and moving when a shriek of terror paralyzed Will.

"Elizabeth Brookley! Elizabeth!" a woman screamed over and over. Will whirled to face the fire as flames burst through a window, lighting a blaze of red-gold hair. "Elizabeth!" he screamed. She hadn't heard. She disappeared through the doorway.

"Stop her! Get her out!" Battling his way forward, his arms flailed out ahead and to the side. He didn't care whom he hit, pushed, trampled. He had to reach her. She was after Eaton's books. Curse the books. Let them burn, but not Elizabeth. O God, not her.

He felt the fire's heat, saw Elizabeth stumble back out the door and drop a pile of books. She turned back and he pushed toward her.

Voices followed him.

"Stop."

"She'll never make it."

"You'll be trapped with her."

Arms reached out. He pulled and thrashed against them. More hands on him, more shouts. He freed one arm and crashed it against the faceless body that restrained him. Now he was caught again, and kicked helplessly to free himself. There she was. More books fell at his feet. Again she disappeared into the flaming building.

Watching the flames light up patches of sky Will stood for a second, then plunged forward. "Let me go." He pulled with strength he did not know he had. He thrashed, he writhed, he bit and suddenly he was free, almost falling forward to face her. She was out.

Her arms were full of books. Her eyes shone. "The least you can do is carry these for me." Her voice quaked and Will swallowed the rush of anger he wanted to shout at her.

That face, streaked with soot, was too small for the eyes in it. Her dress was torn, singed at the bottom, and her hair smelled of smoke.

"Brave girl," he said softly.

Then Elias Eaton was there draping her cloak about her shoulders, thanking, scolding her. Behind them timbers crackled and fell. The splintered smell of wood smoke hung heavy over the dying fire. Glass cracked but slowly now. The crowd milled about hopelessly. Richard Waite stumbled out of the shadow. He grabbed a corner of her cloak, twisted it in his hands and whimpered, "Elizabeth — oh, my God — Elizabeth."

"It's all right, Richard." She patted his hand. "I'm fine."

He straightened up. "Elizabeth, you've made a spectacle of yourself."

Will felt her arm trembling against his. But she spoke to Waite. "Now Master Eaton has family to care for him. Take him home, Richard."

"I'll see you home first."

She seemed not to hear. Her eyes rested on the old man who stood staring at the rubble. His face was empty and his narrow shoulders slumped.

"We'll rebuild it all, sir," Will said. "You'll see."

The man nodded. "Perhaps. In time, perhaps."

"Until then we'll see school is kept." Elizabeth reached for his hand. "Even if we must use a room in my house."

Again he nodded mechanically. He seemed to have no reaction left in him.

"Take him home with you. Please, Richard. Now." She was pleading, a thing Will would not have believed she could ever do.

"I'll see that Elizabeth's safe," Will said.

[77]

Richard hesitated.

"Good night, Richard." This time her voice was firm. She pressed Eaton's hand once again, then quickly walked away.

Will caught up with her. Too tired to talk, they walked side by side across a field toward her house. Mists of warm air swirled over the snow, softening its crust. Their footsteps were soundless.

"What will happen to him?" she asked finally.

Will couldn't answer. It would be a long time before the schoolhouse could be rebuilt. Probably not till the war was over. "Will your father let him use your house?" Will answered with another question.

He felt her stiffen. Whatever she was thinking separated them. They were a few steps from her door but fog, too, came between them. So many times he had wished for just such a chance to talk to her, and now —

"Elizabeth —" he tried to bridge the separation, "Liz —"

Suddenly she whirled to face him. "Shall I use my house for the school?" she demanded. "Of course I shall — as long as it is my house. But how long will it be? You'd know that better than I."

Will stared at her. His face must have reflected the conflict in him. Her eyes softened, but only for a second. "William, I have to know about the petition, and you're the only one I can ask. Will —"

That face, so gentle, so concerned — his breath caught in his throat. He opened his mouth to speak, then clamped it shut. Why me? Why am I the only one you can ask? He stepped back. Do you, too, think me a Tory — or worse, a traitor to my own family? The question raced through his mind.

But Elizabeth's quiet voice continued. "Jonathan overheard Eb Daggett and your brother in the Commons. They were talking about a petition to force anyone loyal to England out of the colony. Father said it was just gossip, but Jonathan thinks it may happen. Mother is frightened and I — I wouldn't have asked you, Will, but after what they did tonight — what next? Are they going to burn us all in our houses? Are they going to make us leave?"

He shut out her voice, but the plea in her face was impossible to avoid. Still, how could he tell her what he had heard tonight? How could he be disloyal to his own family? "Why me? Why ask me?" he blurted.

"Because I know you'll tell me."

She was so sure of herself, so arrogant. He looked away uneasily. "You'd better go inside, Elizabeth," he said gently.

She bowed her head submissively. For a second Will thought he had won. Then she stepped forward, her face tilting up, so close Will could smell the sweetness of her. "Please, Elizabeth, go!"

Were those tears? He refused to see them.

"You *shall* tell me, Will Pinto!"

He almost laughed at her spirit. "No, Elizabeth, I cannot."

Her eyes flashed. "You must."

A sudden shadow of fear washed over her face, and Will's own fright rushed out to meet it. Their thoughts locked like rams' horns in the space between them. "You shall tell me," echoed silently. Why? A race of traitors, is that why? No. Not her. Dear God, not her.

Softly, very softly he said, "How do you *know* I shall tell, Elizabeth?"

"I'm sorry." Pain for him, for herself, for her thoughts, haunted her eyes.

So it was true. Stiff with his own horror he spoke carefully, evenly, "I SHALL NOT TELL YOU."

Was it her own shame that caused her fury? It would be a long time before he could forget her reply. *"Betray your friends, then, and burn for the Jews' everlasting guilt — burn in hell!"*

[Chapter IX]

FROM THAT NIGHT on Will ceased his argument with Jacob. He listened to his father's scorching indictments against tyranny. He felt nothing but sadness when he watched Abraham polish his ensign's braid and military boots that morning before his leaving. Abe and his father simply did not know, would not believe him if he had had the heart to tell them. Wise Jacob, strong Abraham, wily Solomon *did not know* what Elizabeth had told him so plainly — no matter which side any one of them chose, a Jew was still a Jew, to use as firebrand, warrior, friend, informer. Will watched them all and wondered how they managed loyalty to an idea, to a man, to anything but themselves. But with all his sorrow and hurt he felt no bitterness, only a peculiar gratitude for Elizabeth's honesty.

Then Abe was gone, and the winter months lagged. At College he refused to simulate patriotism in exchange for companionship. He was not with them, so most of his classmates assumed he was against them. To the few others he was at best, he knew, suspect. Somehow this pushed him even further away from his father and Solomon.

Each day apprehension was written more deeply in Jonathan Brookley's face. By March the patriots had taken Dorchester Heights and Sir William Howe was forced to evacuate Boston. More than a thousand loyalists fled with the British. The Waites prepared to move to New York. Will ached for the fright he knew all the Brookleys must feel. Once he saw Elizabeth on State Street. Her timid smile brought such a lump to his throat he turned away. After that, as if by spoken agreement, they managed to avoid each other.

School work kept him from his thoughts and during spring recess he threw himself into the shop business with a vigor that amazed, then amused, and then perplexed Jacob. Will cared less than ever about the war. When, in June, Governor Trumbull issued a proclamation of independence for Connecticut, Will didn't even bother to read it. He was numb to the town's excitement, to his father's quiet pleasure as the old man pored over the newspaper's reprint of the document. Sixteen days later, in Philadelphia, the Congress issued a similar declaration. But few people in town took much note of this second paper.

The July heat was trapped in the classroom. So were twelve students. The continuing drone of Mr.

Tutor Timothy Dwight lulled them. Will fixed his eyes on Old Timothy's face and mentally checked off the number of days until the end of classes. Twenty-four, twenty-five, twenty-six, he counted.

A polite knock at the door and Will lost count. Any interruption was welcome, even to Tutor Dwight, the boy suspected. Thirteen newly alert heads turned as one toward the young man in the doorway.

"I'm sorry to interrupt you, Mr. Tutor, sir. I have a message from President Daggett for one of your students, sir." The boy was making the most of the attention suddenly focused on him.

Tutor Dwight waved his hand, graciously agreeing to the messenger's importance. "I'm sure every mind in the room awaits your pronouncements with at least as much eagerness as they await mine." He bowed mockingly.

Uncomfortable laughter rippled softly through the class. No one ever knew when Old Timothy's humor would whiplash into stinging sarcasm.

For a second the messenger looked perplexed. Then, shrugging slightly, he cleared his throat. "President Daggett requests Mr. W. Pinto's presence in the president's office immediately after Master Tutor Dwight dismisses his class."

Whispers hissed through the room. "Tory," Will heard. "— old man'll get him."

The instructor silenced the murmur by lifting an eyebrow. He regarded the messenger who, having delivered himself of his duty, waited, looking questioningly at Mr. Dwight.

"Well said," Dwight congratulated too heartily. "And thank you, sir. I'm confident we comprehend your message to a man."

This time Dwight's sarcasm was not lost on the boy. Hurriedly he retreated.

Dwight watched the boy leave, shook his head, then turned back to the class. "I trust I did not overestimate your ability when I stated you understood Mr. Daggett's message, Mr. Pinto."

Will reddened, but said nothing.

"Well, Mr. Pinto?"

"No, sir."

"Ah, then, every royal fool understood."

There was an audible intake of breath in the classroom.

"Then, go!" the man ordered.

"You haven't dismissed the class — sir."

A pause. Then, "You don't always stick so closely to the rules, do you, Mr. Pinto?" Every man sat straight in his seat. No need to pretend attention now.

"Well, Mr. Pinto?"

"I try, sir."

Another pause, while everyone tried to read the instructor's expressionless face. Timothy Dwight suddenly laughed. "I hadn't noticed."

Will didn't wait to find out what that meant. While Dwight's laughter still echoed, Will retreated.

* * *

Napthali Daggett had never been well liked by the students. Not that they hated him; there was nothing to hate. He was an honest, plodding man, heavy and slow-moving. He pondered his orthodox views seriously and, when the occasion demanded, delivered them in a drawling monotone. Once he made up his mind, as he had on the justice of the revolution, his conclusion was unchangeable.

Will faced him now and searched his own mind. What had he done? More to the point, what had he done that President Daggett could have known about? His mind flashed swiftly — Elias Eaton, that moment with Waite and Brookley, that awful incident in the Chapel. Guilt flushed through him.

Mr. Daggett cleared his throat. Will waited. "Your record has come to my attention, Mr. Pinto."

The old man paused.

"Yes, sir?" Will said, to fill the silence.

The president refused to be hurried. He shuffled some papers and cleared his throat. Finally he said, "I have some questions to ask you."

At least he was going to ask before he accused.

Another long minute. "You are familiar with the Declaration by the Representatives of the United States of America in Congress Assembled?"

Will felt a nerve in his cheek jump and clenched his jaws together. "No, sir."

Mr. Daggett raised his eyebrows, then smiled. "But, of course, you have read it."

"Uh, no, sir, I have not."

Mr. Daggett took his time digesting this news. His

face and tone were somber. "I expected every student should have read it by now. It is a fine document, well phrased, embodying the highest ideals. But it is not too late to make sure everyone in the College is thoroughly familiar with it." He reached for his quill, found a blank sheet, and slowly began to write. Now the only sound in the room was the scratch of pen on paper.

Will wasn't sure if he was expected to wait or to go. He felt prickly little stabs beginning in his left foot, and he curled his toes furiously in his shoe. When that didn't help, he tried forcing all his weight to his right leg. Maybe the old man just wanted to know if he'd read the thing through, he thought, and began to inch back toward the door.

The scratching stopped. Mr. Daggett faced him and Will halted. "I called you in because your tutors have reported — ah-hem —"

What? Will wanted to scream.

"Your tutors feel your penmanship is excellent. I would like you to make a copy of the Philadelphia declaration for me. And Governor Trumbull has requested one also."

Mr. Daggett rose from his chair and walked toward Will, several printed papers in hand. "It is a great honor, Mr. Pinto."

Suddenly Will felt himself trembling. A declaration of independence from England. Could he do this in good conscience? The words were out before he thought. "I'm not sure, sir, I —"

Mr. Daggett smiled. "I respect your humility, my

boy. However, you were chosen for this honor because your elders *are* sure." He held out the papers.

"But —" Will began, and searched for the words. "It's just that I don't believe —"

"Tut, tut, young man, have I not made it plain wiser heads than yours have made the decision? Do not rebuke them with protestations of false modesty." He opened the door, placed the papers in Will's hand, and smiled benignly. "Pen this carefully, several times over, do not hurry. Haste makes waste."

Will found himself outside the closed door.

⌈ Chapter X ⌋

THAT NIGHT, as usual, Abigail moved noiselessly from table to hearth, across the kitchen
and back, carrying an iron pot, then a stack of plates.
Will stared at the bowl of steaming pudding she put
in front of him. Why did she insist on a hot meal
every day? The kitchen was warm enough without
that fire. He wiped his shirt sleeve across his forehead
and glared at Sol. How could he eat in this weather?
Jacob's spoon clicked with maddening regularity
against the pewter bowl. Will shoved his own plate
away from him. If only Sol hadn't come home with
the news of Mr. Daggett's request, if only he himself
had had the courage to tell Mr. Daggett then and
there that he had no intention of copying that paper.
Disgusted, the boy pushed back from the table and
rose.

Jacob smiled up at him. "Going to start work on
the Declaration already?" His eyes shone.

Will looked down. "No. I — I —" He could feel Sol watching him. "Father, I —"

"Yes?" Jacob prompted.

Will's fingers gripped the back of his chair. "I'm not sure I can copy the Declaration."

Jacob held his head to one side. "William, do you appreciate the honor you've been given? President Daggett has asked you to record history." His voice caught on his words.

Sol looked up. He watched Will carefully.

"Father, don't be proud of me, I —"

"Maybe Will doesn't want to copy the Declaration." Sol bent back over his meal.

Jacob laughed. "What gives you such an idea?"

Sol rose, wiped his mouth, then slowly folded his napkin. "Just that Will seems so hesitant."

Jacob ignored the comment. "It's an honor for us all, William. And Abraham will be as pleased as I am." He glanced meaningfully at Sol. "As we all are. But Mr. Daggett was right — don't rush it, son. Do a careful job." He leaned back in his chair and studied Will's face. "I know you shall." He cleared his throat. "Now *I* have some news."

All business, he took an opened envelope from his pocket and briskly smoothed several folded sheets on the table. "It's from my brother Isaac in New York — our annual invitation from the family."

Will couldn't get his mind off the Declaration. I'll have to tell him, he thought. Sooner or later. "I —"

"What does he say?" Will heard Sol's question, but

it was Jacob's answer that brought the boy out of his thoughts.

"He writes the British will soon invade New York, and he's convinced the family must leave." Jacob held the letter up and read:

Our mayor is a venomous Tory, and the royal governor lays off New York in a British vessel, biding the time till he shall return. Many families, convinced the city must become a battleground, have already moved out. Our troops come in daily from neighboring colonies. They work diligently to construct earthworks and barricades. Since the Connecticut forces arrived from Boston, we have been able to see our loved nephew, your son Abraham, only twice. He is well, strong, and of good spirit. So much a mirror of his father I find it hard to credit my own eyes at the sight of him.

Jacob looked away from the letter. "In any case, Isaac has arranged to move the family back to Stratford." He paused. "Thirty years, thirty-five since Isaac left our father's house."

"When will they move?" Sol asked.

Jacob shook his head. "Soon. He's not sure. Still the daily prayers. Isaac. My brother should have been a rabbi," he mused. "But he would like the family to go to Newport in September for Yom Kippur, the holiest day of the New Year service. And if he can arrange it, he wants us to join them there." Tears were in Jacob's eyes.

Will looked at his father. He's getting old, he

thought, and lowered his eyes quickly. He didn't want Jacob to know what he saw.

"It'll mean closing the shop for at least a week, and a hard trip," Jacob continued.

Stunned, Will and Sol gaped at him. "You mean you want to go?"

"But Abigail —" Will looked around for his step-mother. She must have gone to bed without their noticing.

"Yes, I know. I've never gone before because my family wouldn't accept your mother. Even after so many years they have not invited Abigail. But if Newport falls to the British, who knows if I'll have this chance again? Isaac is nearing seventy, and I —"

"It never bothered you before. You always —"

Jacob's eyes silenced Sol. "Each man has thoughts he can't share. You have them."

Sol flushed.

"There's no shame in it, my son. Even fatherhood doesn't abolish the need of privacy." He smiled. "But this I will share — I long more each year for my old customs — though," he added quickly, "I've never thought them better than the next man's. Perhaps it would have cost me less if I had." A moment's thought stopped him.

"In any case, those traditions are the only ones I have. Lately I've realized they're the only ones I have to leave to you. Besides," Jacob broke the intimacy that unexpectedly seemed to embarrass him, "we'll have good news for the family. I do hope Isaac makes the trip definite. They'll all be pleased Will's been

[91]

chosen to copy the Declaration for the Governor of Connecticut and the Yale College records." He rose and reached his arm around Will.

Will drew back, suddenly hating his father. Words sounded in his head, I will not write that declaration of hypocrisy. No matter what he says. I won't. Tell him. Tell him NOW, the room echoed.

He felt his father's insistent arm on his shoulder and heard, "You must know how proud I am of you, my son."

For a moment Will couldn't answer. Then, very softly, he said, "I'm glad for you, Father."

For Will the summer seemed endless. At first, when his father had proposed the trip to Newport, he couldn't believe they would go. Then he became increasingly excited. There were eight aunts and uncles he could not remember meeting, and at least a dozen cousins. There were said to be nearly a hundred Jews in the town of Newport. It was hard to believe. The only Jews he knew were his father, brothers, and himself. How must it feel to go into a church and really belong? He said nothing about his hopes, but each day he raced home to see if there had been any news from Stratford.

The days dragged, and still there was no word from Isaac. At school he waited too. Sooner or later Mr. Daggett would want to see the Declaration. Each time a messenger came into the room, Will stiffened.

It seemed the college, the whole town waited. Wherever he went — Long Wharf, the Green, the marketplace — people waited for news of the invasion of New York.

British strategy was obvious. They would take New York and move up the Hudson to join their Canadian forces. New England would be cut off. Could the rebels prevent this? How? Cobbler, butcher, baker — every man had a different answer while all waited, week after week, for the moment when the right answer must come from George Washington.

Will felt the tension around him, and his own conflict mounted. Why not read the Philadelphia declaration? He did, and was more confused than ever. He couldn't help responding to Jefferson's ideals. In spite of himself, he began to think of the promises the paper held. He even began to copy it. Still he wondered if the equality it promised could ever apply to him. Confused, he switched his thoughts to Newport.

He knew his father's family was well off, and had heard tales of the wealth and style of the Newport Jews. If they did go, would he be able to conduct himself properly? Think about that when the time comes. But how would the family receive him? Did they still resent his gentile mother? Nonsense. How could they? She had insisted on circumcision for her sons. Didn't that make them Jews? Besides, Uncle Isaac had invited him, hadn't he? The boy's spirits soared. They might even meet the famous Aaron López. Perhaps he, who had been denied citizenship in Rhode Island, could explain his loyalty to the United States.

So many answers lay in Newport. If only that letter would come. Perhaps Isaac had changed his mind, didn't want them after all. He refused to let himself think that. Soon. It *would* come soon.

Several times he tried to share his hopes with his brother, but Sol wanted none of it. He would have too much school work to make up, he said, and he had no desire to leave New Haven.

"Aren't you curious about our relatives?" Will asked one night, as he blew out the candle in their room.

"Why should I be?" Sol grumbled. "I've done well enough without them."

"But Father wants it so badly."

Sol punched his pillow angrily. "All of a sudden, after ten years, he's homesick. I think he's gone daft."

"But —" Will began.

"Oh, go to sleep."

So Will kept silent. The weeks of waiting dragged into August. The war news broke first.

The British had taken Long Island. More than eight thousand strong, they landed at Gravesend where Washington had least expected them. New Haven exploded with horrifying reports. Throngs of frightened people filled doorways and streets.

Fear knotted Will's stomach. Abraham. Until now he had denied the possibility that something might happen to Abe. Dodging in and out among the crowd, the boy raced toward home.

"A thousand boys killed."

"Two thousand."

"Our boys are trapped in New York."

Windows flew open and women, their faces white as their caps, called out for more news. Will pushed and shoved his way through the teeming, shouting crowd. If there were any lists of killed or wounded yet, his father would know.

Will felt beads of sweat on his forehead. Voices rang in his ears, but he could make no sense of them. Faces, arms and bodies swirled about, clouded by terrible anger. If Abe was hurt it was Jacob who had done it, Jacob who had sent Abe into this war. And this time his father would have to answer to him.

But Jacob could not. There were no lists. No names. Not yet. Hour after hour went by while they pretended not to wait. Will watched his family and himself go through the motions — rising, eating, drinking, working, sleeping and rising again. Day after agonizing day. Three, four, five, and on the sixth day they knew Abraham was safe.

The next morning Will woke to find Sol's bed empty. He hurried into his clothes, clattered down the stairs, and found his father still at breakfast.

Smiling broadly, Jacob held up a letter. "Our trip to Newport is all settled. We're to meet the family there the third week in September."

Will could hardly believe it all. Abe was safe. They were going to Newport for Yom Kippur. The words had an alien yet strangely familiar sound.

He was late. Sol had already gone, but Will had to know everything. Between mouthfuls of porridge he questioned Jacob. The answers were quick. They were to stay with distant cousins, Moses Hart and his family. The holy day of prayer and fasting began and ended with the last rays of the sun. No one must do any work in the twenty-four hours between. For one night and one day they would forget all worldly and bodily duties and desires, and devote every moment to God.

"Did you tell Sol? That we're going, I mean." Will choked down a last swallow.

"No, he'd gone before —"

Will jumped up. "I'll catch him." He raced out the door. His shoes pummeled the cobblestones. All the way up State Street he ran, rounded the corner and chased till he caught up with his brother on the Green.

"We're going," he panted, falling in step beside Sol. "To Newport."

Sol whirled to face him. "Who says? When?"

"Few weeks," Will breathed heavily.

"Well, I'm not." Sol scowled. "I can't."

"What do you mean — you can't?" Will demanded.

"Just that — I can't." Sol's eyes blazed.

"Why not?" Will felt the anger that rose answering Sol's.

Sol set his jaw. "Where would I say I was going?"

"Oh, I see. You're ashamed to tell your fancy

friends you're going to celebrate the Hebrew New Year."

Sol's hand flew out and grabbed Will's shirt. "Keep your voice down."

"Why should I? It's true, isn't it?" Will grasped Sol's hand and ripped it from his shirt.

Instantly Sol caught Will's wrist and twisted it. "Stop it!"

The stab of pain was infuriating. "You fool — there's not a man in New Haven doesn't know we're Jews."

Sol's face was scarlet. The pulse in his left temple throbbed visibly. "Close your mouth or I'll close it for you." His own voice rose.

Out of the corner of his eye Will could see several people had stopped to watch. One man stood holding his three-cornered hat reverently as he might at a funeral. Mistress Healy came squawking along with her gaggle of geese. Will didn't care. The more he humiliated Sol the better. "You're a Jew and you can't hide from it."

"I'm not hiding from anything. But I won't flaunt a religion I'd never practice." Sol spat the words at him.

"Careful, boy," Will grinned at him. "You're attracting attention. Eb Daggett wouldn't approve of that."

Sol jerked his head nervously around. In that second Will slipped out of his grasp. As he did, the edge of his palm swiped into Sol's arm. Caught off balance, Sol staggered back. An instant's surprise, then fury registered on his face.

Will slashed back blindly. He grazed Sol's shoulder, then missed completely. Furiously he struck again, heard a thud, and winced at the impact in his own arm.

"Let 'm have it."

"Give it to him, boy."

Who were they cheering? Sol was closing in on him. Blow after blow increased in strength. A warm trickle oozed from his nose. He licked at it and lunged.

The crowd roared and stomped their feet.

"That little one's got spirit all right," a voice called.

"That's all he'll have if he don't give in soon," a man guffawed.

He heard Sol groan, then felt the fury of his brother's retaliating punch deep in his belly. Darkness filled the sides of his eyes. The Green seemed to spin around him. Trees dipped toward his face and glided away.

"What's it all about?" someone shouted.

"Who knows? Who cares?" A man laughed. His voice was thin and mean as a snake. "Them Jew boys sure are going at it, though."

"Sol," he tried to say, but his tongue was thick.

His brother's fist crashed into his ears. "Had enough?" Sol hissed venomously.

It was the way he said it that gripped Will's hands tight, kept them moving.

"They'll kill each other," a woman said. "Stop them."

Will reeled and fell. The smell of morning grass mingled with the smell of blood. He lay on his back and watched a cloud of wispy white against blue sky. Sol's face blotted it out. Looming above him, one eye swollen shut, the other a bead of hate, his mouth a tight grimace — was this really Solomon? Struggling beneath Sol's weight, automatically reaching out to claw him, Will didn't know.

"Solomon! William! Oh, my God." Abigail's voice cut through the catcalls, paralyzing Will.

Sol couldn't have heard her. He kept pounding. And then it was over. Will saw nothing but the familiar worn hands clutching Sol's.

She held Sol's hands till Will felt his brother's weight settle heavier on him. The fight had gone out of him.

"Are you all right?" Abigail's head turned quickly from one to the other.

Her hand was cool on his face. For a moment it soothed the ache in his head, then shamed him with its gentleness.

She reached both arms down to raise him. "Help me with your brother, Solomon."

In her voice there was a quiet command, and Sol responded. The crowd muttered as it opened a path for them. She led Will and Sol through it, ignoring the voices.

"They're brothers — could you believe it?"

"Animals, more like," a goodwife sniffed.

Will stiffened. Those hens blamed Abigail. He felt his stepmother's hand tighten on his arm and held his tongue. Sneers and snickers followed them.

"Troublemakers, those Jews, my papa always says," a boy piped.

Taunting boys, sing-songing children, barking dogs tagged behind them in humiliating parade. Across the Green, along the street, around corners they went, and every passerby stopped to watch.

As they entered the door, Will sensed the stragglers waiting, hoping to see more.

[Chapter XI]

WILL KNEW SOL was as ashamed as he was. Somehow their remorse and the fight itself had cleared the air between them. Most of all it was their mutual fear of Jacob's anger that kept them waiting together for his return.

He arrived home early. All that evening he said little, spoke in monosyllables, not once mentioning the fight. The boys shared a terrible sense of dread, and decided the punishment would come at breakfast the next day. By that morning Sol's eye had gone purple-black and his wry grin told Will he too looked less than perfect. Will grinned back and bowed Sol out of their room ahead of him.

"No thanks," said Sol. "After you."

"Together, then," Will suggested.

Sol nodded. Sheepishly they clomped down the stairs.

Jacob was already eating. "You'll both need new

clothes for the trip," he began the minute he saw them. "I'll bring the cloth home at noon, and I think —" he went on and on with detailed plans for their journey.

Eyebrows raised, Sol glanced at Will. With one eye swollen shut, he looked so comical Will almost choked on his laughter.

Jacob didn't seem to notice. Even that night and the next and the one after he said nothing about the fight.

Perhaps he's sensed the change between Sol and me, Will thought. Whatever reason, his father talked only of the trip. Will had never seen him so excited. He traded their old coach and mare for a splendid carriage and two spirited stallions, and he even hired a coachman. His elation was contagious. Abigail hummed as she worked on the fine black broadcloth he brought home. Either Sol was still too repentant to complain or he, too, was caught up in the excitement. Both boys helped Jacob persuade Nathaniel Sloan to manage the shop while they were away. Will went over the ledgers with him one night, Sol the next, then Jacob gave him final instructions. By September 18, the day they were to leave, all three agreed Mr. Sloan might manage to muddle through the week. Abigail closed the trunk and sighed. She could use a week of quiet, she said.

Just as they climbed into the carriage, the post arrived with a letter from Abe. Jacob leaned out of the window to read it to Abigail, but she waved him on.

If Abe had sent the letter, he was well and safe. She'd hear the other news when they returned.

Jacob signaled the coachman and they were off. He settled back and, in spite of the jolts and bounces, gleaned the meat of Abe's letter. The British had indeed invaded New York. Abe's company was part of the force that had helped block the redcoats' advance until Putnam's forces escaped from the city. Then they too managed a safe retreat.

For Will, Abe's safety was all that mattered. But throughout the long, lurching journey, Jacob and Sol planned and replanned an aggressive campaign for General Washington. Will barely heard them. He smiled to himself as the carriage shook and bumped. He was going to a city he had never seen, to meet relatives he could not recall, to pray in a strange temple, and somehow he felt he was going home. They traveled a day and a half, jostled, bounced, and rattled back and forth, while Will dozed and dreamed.

He missed the entrance into Newport, and was still groggy as he walked up the path to the Harts' house.

Tall and imposing, it was every bit as fine as the Waite mansion and freshly painted, with great wooden doors and a knocker so highly polished it captured each ray of afternoon sun. It told of ease within, hinted even of magic. Jacob's fingers barely touched it and the doors swung open in a welcoming arc.

A young woman in maid's black and ruffled white

dropped into a curtsy as pleasant to watch as her smile. "Master Pinto, sir," she said. "The master asked me to show you to your rooms as soon as you arrived."

Jacob hurried them after the girl. Everything happened so quickly — unpacking, washing, changing clothes, then meeting and greeting each newly arrived relative. His father proudly answered all their questions about Abe, and never failed to mention Will was copying the Philadelphia declaration for the Governor of Connecticut. Each time he did, Will noticed Sol's face tighten.

Will felt more than saw the elegance around him, and not until they were seated at the long dinner table did he begin to connect the twenty-odd names and faces.

Directly across from him sat a man with a scholar's thin face and seeking eyes. His shoulders hunched as if his dinner plate were a book — Uncle Joseph Pinto, the one who never married. On his right was Aunt Rachel, two years older than Will's father but still touchingly pleased by her own undeniable beauty. Her features were delicate, her oil-smooth skin only faintly lined, and lighted by silver waves in a coil of black hair. And on his left was Uncle Solomon, named, as was Will's brother, for a great-grandfather Will had never known and suddenly now wondered about. The boy glanced at each of the five oil portraits that hung on the dining room walls. He must ask Jacob about that old Solomon later.

Now he scanned the room. To the left was a large

bay window and on the floor lay a great Oriental carpet. A vast damask cloth covered the oval table. Each place was laid with a chilly white plate, gadroon edged and exquisitely emblazoned in gold. High glass goblets cut in baroque designs made rainbows from the reflection of gleaming silver. A wine-colored epergne piled with oranges, dates, pomegranates and cascading grapes stood in the center of it all.

More unbelievable than any of the grandeur was the warmth. In their voices, their color, their eyes, their gestures, the Pintos offered the richness of themselves to each other and the newcomers. Will saw the pleasure they took in the taste, smell and touch of their possessions. He sensed that their enjoyment in the fruit of the earth and the vineyard and their own labor was, for them, a celebration of God. It was all so different from New Haven, where any pleasure seemed faintly wicked.

He looked to Uncle Isaac Pinto for the answer. Without doubt the table centered around him. His face was thin and lined, his voice cracked with age. But there was a strength in him. Perhaps it was the way he held his head erect, perhaps the wisdom in his eyes, or the knowledge of many years. It was Isaac who rose to offer the prayer.

Laughter trailed off, voices rushed sentences to quickly whispered ends. Two serving girls backed hastily out of the dining room.

"Ssh," Aunt Rachel held her finger to her lips, cautioning her small grandson.

The boy's eyes, shiny as a badger's, fastened on Uncle Isaac.

Four other cousins stiffened to attention. "I didn't have to be told," a starched young miss whispered loudly.

Isaac looked at their host, Moses Hart, and noted the empty chair next to him.

"My niece has been delayed," Mr. Hart said. "She'll join us as soon as she can." He smiled apologetically. "So young to run a household. But a most capable girl."

Uncle Isaac nodded. He took up his prayer book.

Chairs creaked as bodies settled back. Isaac waited till not even the tinkle of crystal could disturb the blessing. He raised his wine glass, smiled at them all and began the Hebrew chant.

The other men, wearing skullcaps similar to Isaac's, followed the blessing in their books.

It was a stirring song, a kind of ancient Eastern music that reached inside Will and set chills trembling through him. He looked across the wide table at his father. Jacob's head bent forward over the prayer book, his lips silently formed the strange words, and his body, like the twelve other men's, swayed gently back and forth. Watching him was like watching a stranger.

The boy turned quickly to his brother. Sol's eyes had fastened on Jacob with a look of disdain that shocked Will. But before he could be sure, the look was gone.

And blessed art Thou
O Lord our God
Who created the
Fruit of the vine.

The melodic chant ended. In the reverent silence
that followed the men drank deeply. The ritual wine
was sweet and thick in Will's mouth. Its aroma mingled with the foreign spice smells that drifted from
the kitchen. Will felt the air, warm, like balm on his
face.

He saw his father looking over the rim of his glass
toward Sol and him. Was the satisfaction on Jacob's
face marred by guilt? Was he ashamed? Could it be
because he's never shared his religion with us, Will
wondered.

Soft footfalls broke the silence. Mr. Hart rose,
smiling, "Ah, an answer to a prayer." He reached
out to the girl who entered. "May I present my niece,
Rebecca?"

Will felt his eyes widen. He had managed to believe this room and these people were not a dream.
But the girl — he couldn't take his eyes off her.

A finger jabbed his back. He jerked around. Sol
grinned down at him. Every man in the room was
standing. Flushing furiously, Will stumbled up.

"Please sit down, gentlemen," Rebecca said.

The thick rug muffled the scrape of chairs, con-
versations resumed. Silver clattered against china.
Wine gurgled from decanter into glass. Serving girls

passed heavy platters. But Will couldn't move. He knew he was staring. How could anyone not? That face, that cloud of dark hair framing it, that skin — all so warm and rich with color. He watched her nod from one guest to another, and his breath caught in his throat. A princess — a princess with eyes rich and black as ripe olives.

"Rebecca," Will heard her uncle say, and the sound of the name surged warmly through him.

"You must eat, William." Aunt Rachel's voice was soft. "There won't be another chance until tomorrow sundown."

Will nodded and blushed. He turned his attention carefully to the meal. One course rivaled the next in splendor. He had never tasted such food — beef ground tender and wrapped in grape leaves, duckling that glistened and smelled of oranges, dates stuffed with nuts, tiny thin-crusted pastry oozing honey and crushed almonds.

On and on came the food, the talk. Will was dazed. But the sun was beginning to go down. Aunt Miriam rose. "It's time we left for the synagogue," she said gently.

Everyone stood. Will felt a hand on his shoulder.

"Come, it's time to go," his aunt whispered.

Reluctantly, and still bemused, Will pushed his chair back and mechanically followed the others to the door.

Outside, the shock of cold was a relief. Startled by the brisk, clean evening air and the street teeming with sailors, farmers, goodwives, and merchants he was himself again, Will Pinto. He smiled. Odd to be surprised at the sight of homespun. The wine must have gone to his head. Or was it the dinner with all its courses, the elegance of the house, the new relatives, the girl Rebecca, that had lulled his mind with a daze of sensation?

It was a short, steep walk uphill to Jeshuat Israel, the synagogue. Will walked silently along with Sol behind their father and Uncle Isaac. Little time to sort out his feelings now.

The sun, behind them, slipped beneath the bay's horizon, shading the wooden building to tones of gray. Beyond the two tall columns of the thronged entry, heavy double doors opened into the synagogue. Will followed his father through the decorous crowd. Voices lowered as they approached. Will sensed something missing, unaware just what.

He stepped into a burst of candlelight illuminating order, harmony, and solemnity. Inside he saw Sol's hand reach for his hat, then slide back to his side. Jacob had warned them both they must keep their heads covered in the synagogue in respect to the Hebrew custom. The brothers' eyes met in a shared moment. Will's training, too, urged him to remove his hat. Both boys stuck close to their father's heels.

Now Will faced the altar on the far wall and saw the royal purple velvet curtains that protected the Ark. It held the ten commandments and the Torah — the holy books. In front and to the right of the sacred scrolls was the pulpit, facing several rows of seats.

Directly behind the pews, in the center of the room, stood a square platform, handsomely railed and cornered by four finely wrought glowing candelabra. It set off the muted colors of an exquisite tapestry that draped a large inclined stand. Just above it another more magnificent candelabrum hung suspended from the great ceiling. Ionic columns on the sides and toward the front of the spacious room supported a deep gallery. Looking up toward it, Will's eyes were caught by the colorful clothes of the women who sat in the gallery. He looked around for a stairway and, finding none, realized the women must have come in a separate entry. Under the gallery were more seats, nearly all darkened by the somber elegance of black-suited gentlemen.

After the Pintos had been ushered to their seats, two men in long robes mounted the platform stairs. Long white shawls covered their shoulders and hung nearly to the floor. One wore a miter-shaped white hat, the other a larger black one.

"That's the Reverend Mr. Touro and the man in white is the cantor," Jacob whispered to his sons.

The prayers began and dark fell richly against the temple windows. Will wound the embroidered scarf, the tallith, about his shoulders. Its silken length warmed him with the richness of his father's faith. The synagogue surged with praise of a God whose mercy had parted a sea. The congregation implored forgiveness. They wept for their own sins in a temple they had built with an escape passage. His father had told him it was there. Who knew when another

Pharaoh, another Inquisition, could rise? Would their God ever let them rest?

Will's blood pulsed to the rhythm of the ancient blessings and his mind groped for understanding. Who was this Elohim whose omnipotence managed such devotion while His chosen still wore His scars? Wasn't He the author of their harm? How could they glorify Him?

Will wondered as he watched his father touch the prayer shawl to his lips and heard himself repeat words he must once have known.

> *Hear, O Israel,*
> *The Lord, Our God, The Lord*
> *Is One.*

The cantor sang, weeping long gone but still remembered pain. The elders swayed to the chant before the Ark. Will began to taste the bitterness of their affliction. He was adrift, needing something he had never known. He wanted to accept the religion of his forefathers. But to do so meant to accept a God who could be angry as well as loving. His mind sagged with the dilemma until the chant of the Kol Nidre began.

The majesty of their supplication stirred his soul till he, too, felt a surge of passion for that God who chose the Jew and promised Canaan.

Later, outside, the moon shone full on Newport, lighting the streets. Standing next to Sol at the gate,

Will saw his father slowly helping Isaac down the stairs. Then in the full dark light Jacob's face appeared, eased and unguarded as Will had never seen it. Joy leaped exultantly in the boy. His father felt as he did, that they were home at last.

[Chapter XII]

WILL'S HAPPINESS and sense of belonging was undiminished the next morning. As he waited outside the synagogue for the day's service to begin, he smiled broadly and greeted everyone in sight, even people he hadn't met.

A portly, red-faced gentleman marched by. Will beamed. "Good morning, sir."

Puzzled, the man stared at Will through his small spectacles. Then he moved his head back till his several pink chins rested on his white collar. He studied Will without recognition. "Ah, hm, yes — good morning." He took out a handkerchief and mopped his brow. "Warm day. Yom Kippur always warm." He touched his hand to his hat and moved on. In a second he was back, his face creased into a dozen gleeful wrinkles. "Master Pinto — from New Haven," he said triumphantly.

"Yes, sir." Will nodded heartily.

A lady in a silk bonnet nodded back.

Will beamed. Now he could understand the ease of Zeph Swift, Webster, Brookley, Waite and the others. It's like this for them every day. Every day of their lives they belong as I belong here.

Dazzled by his discovery, his spirits soared still higher.

People were moving toward the temple doors behind him and for a moment the gateway was empty. A sudden flurry of red filled it. The plumes of her hat curling gracefully about her face, her hand resting on her uncle's arm, Rebecca turned onto the path.

With a flush of pleasure Will headed toward her. "Excuse me. Excuse me, please." He stepped in and around the worshipers to intercept her as she moved toward the women's entrance.

"Good morning."

She stepped back, then laughed, "You startled me."

In that instant and for that laugh Will adored her. His mood blanketed all prudence. "Do you ever come to New Haven? Could you?" he asked.

Gleaming, her eyes responded. Still she hesitated, appraised Will thoroughly, then said, "Perhaps. But first you must speak with my uncle."

For a second he stared at her. All he meant was that he'd like to see her if she came to New Haven, get to know her. "I — I," he stammered.

She lowered her eyes. "My uncle's quite easy to

[114]

talk to, and very possibly he'd approve." She had mis-interpreted his silent surprise as timidity.

Utterly tongue-tied with shock, Will let himself move away from her, with the crowd, into the synagogue. Elizabeth would never have misread him so completely. Elizabeth always knew. He shook his head. But Elizabeth did not belong here — as surely as his mother never had, nor Abigail.

From his seat on the left he could see Rebecca in the front row of the gallery. He watched her lips move easily to form the strange Hebrew words. Beyond a doubt she belonged. If she should marry, wouldn't her husband be accepted equally? His ears stopped hearing the religious chant as he considered this. Yes, he was certain he would be. And Rebecca was, indeed, beautiful. A wife a man could be proud of.

It wasn't too soon for him to think about marriage. He'd probably graduate in another year. Then he'd find a job, and after that he'd be ready to take a wife. Still, two years at best until he could belong someplace — it seemed an eternity.

He glanced at his father. Jacob wore the same ease Will had seen the night before. The man's eyes warmed to each new prayer. Maybe *now* Jacob might consider coming back to the family. Will hugged the hope tight inside him.

The Reverend Mr. Touro mounted the pulpit for the sermon. Will saw his father settle comfortably back. Sol, too, relaxed. This portion of the service would be in English.

The rabbi's greeting was short, but the rest of his speech dragged. Will felt his eyelids grow heavy, and for the first time he thought of the breakfast he had missed. His father began to doze, and Sol slumped further back into his chair.

It was the word "rebellion" that shook him awake. ". . . rebellion against our gracious King who, in England itself and in the colonies, has subjected us to few disabilities." Will felt Sol stiffen next to him. He was afraid to look at his father, nor could he listen to more. Every word Mr. Touro uttered was a hammer crashing at his hopes for Jacob's return to the family.

Will heard the angry explosion of breath next to Sol, could almost feel the heads turning, the necks that craned in indignation. The boy gripped his fists tight. He looked up toward Rebecca. She listened to the rabbi politely. His eyes sought Moses Hart. Then he heard the rasping loudness of a chair pushed back. Another scrape and Will knew, without looking, it was from his father and Solomon. Sol, looking triumphant, motioned Will to follow. Will's mouth went dry, but he refused to look at his brother. From the corner of his eye he saw Sol's smirk as he moved out after their father. Will licked his lips. They were leaving the synagogue. On this Most Holy of Holy Days Jacob Pinto was walking out of the temple. Mr. Abraham Rivera rose next. Then Mr. Aaron López followed by Uncle Isaac Pinto.

Will caught his breath. Moses Hart's forehead

creased with annoyance, but he kept his eyes intent on Rabbi Touro and nodded his agreement.

Stubbornness glued Will to his chair. Embarrassed by the empty seats around him and ashamed of his disloyalty to his father, still he stayed. He looked around, trying to focus his anger. Rebecca sat up there in her fancy clothes, her bland gaze never straying from the rabbi's face. Doesn't she know what's going on? Or doesn't she care? He shot her a venomous glance. She didn't notice. Her hands properly folded in her lap, she stared straight ahead. Does she stay because of her uncle or because she herself agrees with the rabbi? Most probably because it would be incorrect to leave, Will thought savagely.

The rest of the service was a blur of hopelessness and fear of his father's anger.

At sunset, walking back to their house with Master Hart and Rebecca, Will was miserable. His head ached and his stomach growled. He tried to keep his mind on Master Hart's polite conversation and Rebecca's banter but it was useless. Jacob could never be part of all this. It's his blasted war that ruins everything. Will kicked a stone in their path.

"What's the matter? Hungry?" Rebecca laughed. "I am, too. On Yom Kippur I can never think about anything but supper from noon on."

Will didn't bother answering. They were approaching the house.

Once inside at the table he couldn't look at anyone. Plainly his father was making everyone uncomfortable. Aunt Rachel chatted nervously throughout the meal. Aunt Miriam and the other women did their best to help her avoid any controversial talk. Uncle Isaac said little. Even the children sensed something that made them hold their tongues. And Jacob, though he took part in the prayers, made it clear he remained only to break the fast with the family. As soon as he decently could, after supper ended, he thanked his hosts and made haste to leave.

It was too soon, too quick to leave them, but Sol shot him a single glance and Will knew he had no choice.

Everyone filed out after him. Uncle Joseph shook his hand, Aunt Miriam kissed him, Uncle Solomon put his arm round him and when Aunt Rachel hugged him and told him to come back as soon as he could Will blinked hard. While the cousins crowded about with sticky faces waiting to be kissed, Will saw Rebecca slip out the door. He knew he must follow.

She was waiting outside on the stoop. He could barely see her in the darkness. "I'm sorry there wasn't more time," he said, and felt his own stiffness.

"You could write. I'd answer. We'd know each other that way." She paused, then rushed on, "I might visit New Haven, but it's fair to tell you I could never live so far from my people."

Will nodded. He respected her forthrightness, but wished she could have understood he knew that. Actually, he wouldn't want her anywhere but here. "Or your synagogue," he added for her.

"Yes." In the uneasy silence he suddenly thought of another Jewess, Ruth was it? ". . . for whither thou goest, I will go; and where thou lodgest, I will lodge; thy people shall be my people, and thy God my God."

He must have spoken aloud for her answer came quickly. "First thee must know thy God and thy people."

He smiled. She was a sensible girl who came quick to the meat of the trouble. He liked her. Maybe that was enough.

The great wooden doors opened, flooding light on them. Jacob strode out of the house, followed by Sol and Uncle Isaac.

His father refused to look at him now, as he had all during the meal. Nor did he call, but the summons was clear.

"I'll write," Will said, and in the second before he turned he was rewarded with a smile too exquisite to forget. He hurried after his father.

Uncle Isaac held the coach door open for him. Will climbed in and stepped carefully over his father's feet to the middle seat. Before he settled in, the door banged shut.

Isaac looked up at Jacob through the open coach window. "Don't condemn us all for Mr. Touro's sermon. Except for Moses Hart and Myer Pollack, I understand the entire congregation was angered by the rabbi's speech."

"Then why do they tolerate him?" Jacob snapped.

Isaac's tone was gentle, his eyes warm as burnished wood. "Those who remained to listen did so out of respect for his calling."

"Then your leaving indicates you do not regard your religion so highly as your constant chanting implies?"

Will heard the quick sound of shocked disbelief that came from Sol. He too was shocked that their father would speak so to his eldest brother. But Will knew that though Jacob was disgusted with the rabbi and the congregation, his real anger had been ignited by Will's refusal to walk out of the temple. The boy wished he could somehow explain this to his uncle.

Isaac lowered his eyes, then reached out, groping for his words and Jacob's hand. "Perhaps I regard my brother and my principles more highly than I should." Softly he said, "God forgive me. And may He protect you, Jacob."

"And you, Isaac." He had softened momentarily for the farewell. But as he ordered the driver ahead, his voice was angry.

They swung around the corner of High Street onto Griffin and the coach candle threw a brief light across Jacob's face. In that instant Will was afraid.

Will, Solomon, and Jacob sat in a huddle of taut silence. Even the horses' hooves clattered wrathfully against the cobblestones. The furious sounds mounted in intensity as, reaching the outskirts of the city, they increased in velocity. Will could almost feel the volume of his father's rising anger crowd against him in the small coach.

The more he shrank from it, the more stifling the

silent fury became. Suddenly he sat upright, flexing his elbows outward, claiming his rightful place on the narrow seat. He jostled Sol.

"What the devil —" Sol began.

"Sorry," Will said tersely.

"Sorry?" Jacob demanded.

And the boy knew it had begun. Let the old man say what he would. Will was waiting, almost eagerly, to answer him.

"Typically inconsiderate — lack of respect — humiliate your own father — sit and drink in that loyalist drivel."

"I intended no disrespect to you, sir."

"Then what did you intend?"

"To show my respect for a congregation that welcomed us as none ever has."

"Even if in doing so you refute your own principles?"

Will took a deep breath, and exhaling slowly, wondered how it had come to this. "Perhaps I was not refuting *my* principles but *yours*."

"What?" Jacob did not seem to believe he had heard correctly.

"I don't believe the Reverend Mr. Touro's sermon *was* drivel. In fact, he made good sense."

Horrified, Jacob leaned forward to look at Will. He seemed unable to believe the words he had plainly heard. "You cannot mean this." A statement had been intended, but in the telling a question was finally asked.

Will knew his father had begun to believe for the first time what Sol and the others had so long suspected.

"All the man said was why rebel against a King who has put so few restrictions on us? Why, Father? Why should we?"

"It is your youth that shortens your sight, William. We live well now by the tolerance of this King's mood. Chance, greed, anything may alter that mood as swiftly as the wind changes — then what? I will fight to guarantee my rights, and yours, and those of your children."

"And spill blood for a piece of paper? How many pieces of paper burned in the flames of the Inquisition?"

"You copied the Philadelphia declaration. Did you read it?"

"I read it, Father. The words are lofty and so, I believe, are the intentions of those who wrote them. But those men are human as George III, and chance, mood, greed can move them as easily. It is fine for the Englishmen, perhaps even the Dutch, the French, and the Spaniards — but for us, Father? Take off your blinders. Whether or not we pray in the synagogue or observe the dietary laws, are friends to our neighbors and fight in their army, or marry their women — we are Jews, Father. And when we least expect it, they will remind us."

The carriage lunged sideways, flinging Jacob forward. The boy squelched his impulse to help him regain his balance. Let him fall, Will's fury told him.

It was Solomon, so unnaturally silent, who had to twist in his seat to catch their father. Obviously aware of Will's feeling, the man pointed his finger at him. His face flamed with rage.

"Don't you dare whine about prejudice. Fight against it."

"Fight when there's no hope of winning?" Will lashed out his answer.

"Yes," Jacob hissed. "Live like a man."

The coach careened into a sudden road rut, jerking them all forward. This time the man grabbed furiously at the side rope. He clutched it with both fists as if to strangle Will's stubbornness.

A long, awful silence followed. The rage between Will and his father swelled till it seemed to blot out Sol. There wasn't space for anything but anger.

How, thought Will, could his father be so stupid? "How," he demanded, "can you fight for freedom alongside men who own slaves? Freedom for only some — surely even you must admit that is impossible."

But Jacob would not. "Then slavery will go," he insisted.

"Or freedom for more and more people will. I *refuse* to fight for such a doubtful cause."

Their argument grew, gnawing into the night, until Will saw fury distort his father's features. A vein in his forehead beat out against his skin, throbbed his anger as loudly as his words. "Share my fight or leave my house!"

⌈ Chapter XIII ⌋

NO OTHER WORD was spoken all that long trip back to New Haven. Then there had been several days of silence. Will would continue to live at home until graduation and he must decide whether or not he would enlist.

At first life was almost bearable because he hurled himself headlong into an attempt to graduate with Sol's class in February.

Obviously amused and convinced Will couldn't possibly complete the requirements by then, Sol was willing to help. "No, no, that's wrong. Let me show you." Looking over Will's shoulder as he struggled with Divinity and Ethic or Newton's *Principia,* Sol pointed out his errors. But each day's diligence became each week's success, and Solomon's aid grew less frequent. Jacob was pleased. Somehow he seemed to think Will's progress at school indicated the boy had regained his lost senses.

The minute their father offered Will a word, even a glance, Sol was provoked. His jibes at the "bookworm" eventually became sly attempts to strip bandages from a hidden sore. "Hope I'll be assigned right after graduation. The sooner the better. Do you think I'll be with Abe's regiment, Father? If only Will would —"

"He will make the right decision." For the second time that he could remember, Will felt his father's arm on his shoulder.

Every fiber of mind and muscle yearned to return that stern caress, every instinct urged him to reach out toward the man. Yes, Father, yes, I will follow you. What cursed stubbornness stilled his tongue? Please, Father, please, another gesture, another word. His mind begged in silence. And now Jacob, as though similarly damned, stepped back.

It seemed to Will they had never lived any other way, so close to the edge of disaster they were forced to avoid each other for days. Still each day pressed upon the next, pushing him toward decision.

He stayed in the College Library each night until it closed, then walked until he was sure his father and Sol were asleep.

Tonight he walked again. Past the college gates, across the Common, through the mist-heavy evening, painfully alone outside the lighted houses. Hurrying away from them, he headed toward Long Wharf and the sea. It would be all gray there, sky, ocean empty, with no homely sights or smells to tantalize. Now, approaching the tawny marsh reeds, he wondered how he could force himself to fight a war he found absurd. And if he couldn't, would he ever be able to explain to Abe? How could he tell his brother he despised the rebels' killing as much as he hated the King's? One army or another, what difference? New York had been as plagued by the demands of the Continental Army as it now was by the British. And each army ravaged its own men with hunger and cold. What reason explained such destruction? He detested it all and himself because he could not find, believe, or accept *any* answer.

On the path, he followed the flat lands stretching seaward. Hip high and brown, grass waved listlessly beneath the soundless wind and weighted clouds. The meadow's mood matched his own. If in the next months he still could not resign himself to war, then what? His father's anguish, Abe's disdain — could he bear it? Where could he go? To the Tories because they did not fight? The possibility existed, it *was* an alternative. He could go to Newport. His own relations had gone back to Stratford, but Rebecca was still there, the synagogue, too. He would find work. Or rather, he smiled, she would find him work. *There was* comfort, and his soul ached for it. Still, was that all he wanted? Yes. No. Oh, God, where do I belong?

A single gull dipped and soared, his cry aborted by a crashing sea. Suddenly he wanted no more of this emptiness. Turning, he ran. Back to the brightening village lights, back to the sounds of life.

He chose the longest way round to State Street. It

was still too early to go home. He smelled roasting goose, the fruit-nut heaviness of pudding and the warmth of rum long before he heard the roistering tavern sounds. Approaching the Cork and Bottle, he slowed his gait, wanting to savor it all. But inside they would be talking about the British seizure of Fort Washington. — The battle hadn't lasted two hours, and nearly three thousand rebels were taken prisoner. Abe had written home about it. Will sighed and walked past the tavern. Across the Green he recognized Zeph Swift and Webster in a group of his classmates. Hurriedly, he turned the corner.

Past the Talmadge house, the deserted Waite mansion, the Brookleys', he went. The Eaton cottage glowed an invitation to him.

The door opened long enough for Will to see three boys leave. Since the fire, Master Eaton kept school in his house, and though he was the only master in New Haven, there were few enough pupils for a suspected Tory. But only three. No, it was late. The others must have gone earlier.

He hadn't realized how much he missed the old schoolmaster until he met his pleased welcome. He ushered Will inside, questioning the boy's health, his studies, almost boasting his own good fortune tonight. "Not one, but two visitors this evening. My assistant is here."

"Elizabeth." Will felt his voice catch in his throat. He barely heard Master Eaton.

"With all the young men going off to war, there's no one to replace me." The master led Will into the company room. "Nothing like a paucity of employees to insure one's employment."

She sat at the oak table, her head bent. Her hair spilled over her shoulders, almost touching the papers and books spread out in front of her. As they entered she looked up. Will caught the quick pink flush that colored her face. But her gaze was steady. "How are you, Will?" She really wanted, waited for, his answer, her eyes assured him.

"I'm well, Elizabeth. And you?" He never dreamed he could show her the warmth his voice betrayed. Always, in his reveries, he had been cold, snubbing her overtures until she asked his forgiveness. Now, facing her, it was he who longed for her pardon.

As though she had read his mind she smiled, and her face caught the light in her hair.

Remembering her so well, he had forgotten the smile that set his blood racing. "Elizabeth —" he began, then suddenly remembering what she had said that night after the fire, he clamped his jaws tight.

"Sit down, my boy, sit down." Mr. Eaton waved him vaguely to a chair his eyes did not trouble to focus on.

Pride stiffened the boy's spine. "I don't want to interrupt. I'll come back another time."

"Nonsense. Miss Brookley and I have long finished our work. You're interrupting nothing."

Elizabeth gathered the papers into a neat pile and put a paperweight on top. "I'm just waiting for Jonathan. He'll be here to fetch me shortly."

Still Will could not sit.

For a moment no one moved. Master Eaton, sensing some meaning in the stiff silence, looked bewildered.

"Shall I make a pot of tea?" Elizabeth rose without waiting for an answer. Then brushing by him she whispered, "You baby!"

"Thank you, my dear. Tea would be lovely." Elias Eaton rubbed his gnarled hands, then settled back apparently warmed just by the thought of his cup. "You know, William, it's fortunate you came by this evening. I had just been thinking about you." He sucked his pipe. "Today I had a letter from a Groton gentleman requesting the name of a bright young man who might be interested in teaching grammar school starting in February."

The gentle eyes sought above the spectacles for Will's response. Finding none, he said, "I thought of you immediately. You'd make a fine schoolmaster, and I do believe you would enjoy the work." The old head turned toward the books scattered on the table. "A life not without rewards." Then he turned back to Will. His cheeks seemed to sink deeper into his skull and his lips narrowed in resignation. His voice went flat. "But I suppose you have come to tell me you are following your brothers to the army."

"NO." The force of his answer shocked the boy even more than the master. Relief overwhelmed him. His old teacher, as so many times before, had led him to his own truth. Fearful lest a change of heart send him back into uncertainty, he plunged on. "I'll be happy to take the Groton job. Please let them know right away, sir. Tonight. I'll post the letter for you. Shall I get you pen and paper?"

The tea tray tinkled. Will had no choice but to help Elizabeth. He took the tray from her, carried it across the room to the table, and set it down. He waited to give Master Eaton his cup, looking down at Elizabeth as she poured. For the first time he noticed the scatter of freckles on the bridge of her nose. No question, she wasn't beautiful. Not like Rebecca. He watched her capable hands move swiftly. Not a patch on Rebecca. But as she handed him the cup a wave of tenderness filled him.

Her smile was instant. Undoubtedly she sensed what he felt. Will took his own cup without looking into her face.

Luckily Master Eaton was in a talkative mood. He sipped his tea, rocked in his chair, and reminisced about his days as a young teacher. He remembered old satisfactions and offered Will the benefit of them. He told him what he might expect in Groton. They were no longer master and pupil. There had been a subtle change. Will became a colleague. Welcoming him as such, Master Eaton included him in a society of men too civilized for war. Elizabeth, too, seemed a member of this group and their approval, tinged as it was with unspoken censure of Jacob and Abraham, discomfited him. Still, since he must begin to face the consequences of his decision, why not accept its rewards? Prompting Mr. Eaton into further reveries, he settled back to enjoy the old man's stories and almost succeeded in basking in Elizabeth's esteem. Yet somehow in the back of his mind was a nagging thought. He wasn't sure he wanted her esteem if it had to be based on tonight's decision.

Later, walking home, he realized that facing Jacob would be another matter. He would wait. No need to tell him right away. He must give himself a chance to word his arguments carefully, choose a time when he could talk to his father alone. It would be some evening after the meal when Abigail cleared the kitchen and Sol was at his studies. No, not then. Bad news was always worse at night.

He planned and re-planned in his bed, unable to lie still, unable to move lest he wake Solomon and blurt the news that grew each moment into a nightmare of fear and guilt. Anxiety stabbed at him and doubt lurched in his stomach. By morning, his head ached and his throat was too dry to speak. I'll tell him after breakfast, he thought, but did not. At day's end he had convinced himself he wouldn't say anything until February.

That evening his father read aloud a new letter from Abe. Though the war wasn't going well, Abe always managed to report some American triumph, even if it was just, like tonight's letter, the confiscation of three British pigs. Will could not bear the sweetness of Jacob's delight in each word.

Abigail, glancing at Will's face, heaped his plate, urged him to eat. But each mouthful he took from his father's table fell leaden into his stomach.

Smiling, Jacob put down the letter. "Any other news?"

If only he had not asked that question. If only Sol had had some ready answer or Abigail had not looked at Will expectantly. If only Will had not been cursed with his father's respect for the truth.

Will squared his shoulders and faced Jacob. "I've made my decision." He watched the blood drain from his father's face, saw Abigail's hand flutter to her chest, felt Sol's attention fasten on him. They waited.

The hope in that silence chilled the boy. He had to speak. "I —" his voice was a squeak. He stopped, cleared his throat, began again. "I am going to teach school in Groton."

"Not the army?" His brother's gasp was hushed. Even Solomon could not believe the treachery his taunts had implied.

Abigail's face was a blank of disbelief.

Jacob roared his pain. "I DO NOT BELIEVE IT."

"It's true, Father."

"I do not believe it," Jacob echoed himself.

Will gripped the edges of his chair and forced himself further. "I can't believe in your war and I can't fight it. It's no use for me to pretend to myself I can."

"Then you will not fight for your people or your country?" Jacob's voice was hollow, his eyes wet.

"If they were my people, if this were my country —".

"*Not* your people — your country?" he thundered. "I am your father, they are my people, their cause my cause. If you be traitor to them, then," tears fell into the furrows of his face, "be you traitor to me."

Beyond ordinary anger, his voice crashed, "The thunderings and the lightnings, and the voices of the horn and the mountain smoking." From Jacob trembled the wrath of Jehovah.

Thy beauty, O Israel, upon thy high places is slain!
How are the mighty fallen!

Tell it not in Gath,
Publish it not in the streets of Ashkelon;
Lest the daughters of the Philistines rejoice,
Lest the daughters of the uncircumcised triumph:

He cried out his shame, then turned to face Will. "Traitor to me, to mine — no son of mine. I curse the rotten seed that sired you." He raised his right hand, ripped the shirt cloth above his heart, and keened, "O my son Absalom, my son, my son Absalom! would I had died for thee, O Absalom, my son, my son!"

For his father, Will was dead.

He still heard, could feel, the sound of ripping cloth. Numb with horror, he let Sol lead him to their room. There he stood bewildered, seeing his room through a long hall of time. Sitting on the bed seemed an offense to its owner, Jacob. And Solomon, standing there almost in awe of him, was, if not a stranger, then a shadow of memory. Should he pack his clothes, leave now? By his act of mourning, Jacob had made him dead.

"Sit down, Will," Solomon said.

The boy obeyed.

"Take off your shoes."

Again Will complied. He watched his brother turn down the bed and accepted Sol's assumption he was to stay the night. He saw the brotherly kindnesses and felt neither gratitude nor sorrow that this concern had come too late.

"Do you want to talk about it, Will?" His voice was taut with uncertainty.

"No," Will answered.

A pause. Then, "Sure?"

"Yes."

Another moment or two or five. "Then go to sleep. It will be different in the morning."

Will lay back. Maybe.

"Good night, Will."

He was too numb to answer.

But in the morning it was no different. Jacob never once spoke to Will, did not seem even to see him. His father wore the ripped shirt for the traditional Hebrew week of mourning. He closed the shop, and each sunrise and sunset recited the Kaddish, the prayer for the dead.

Yis-gad-dal v'yis-kad-dash sh'meh rab-bo —

Will heard it all, watched his father's face, and somehow felt obliged to stay on until time had gone, graduation was over, and his bags packed.

He could see the farewell pained Abigail and Solomon, and he was surprised. For him there was no pain left. No joy, no regret. When Abigail reached out her arms to wish him godspeed, he felt her face against his cheek, and thought this was the first time anyone had touched him since that night he felt Jacob's arm on his shoulder. There was no joy in the touch, no regret.

He shook Solomon's hand, saw his remorse, knew it stemmed partly from useless guilt, but could not care enough to reassure him.

"You'll write to us, Will?" Abigail asked.

"Yes." It was as easy to say as "no," though he had little idea he ever would.

"Good-bye, William."

"God be with you, child."

He came to Groton as he had left New Haven, empty.

Chapter XIV

HE WAS TO BOARD in a cottage facing the Green, two houses from the school. A widow, Mrs. Thomas, owned it, kept it scrubbed of warmth, and daily provided two tasteless meals. In Will's room there was a bed, a chest, a chair, and the hollow scent of emptiness. It was welcome. There was little risk he would care or be cared about here. He could do his work and let time have its way with him.

The school, a single room smaller than Master Eaton's, was much the same — hard-back chairs, slates, a few maps, wooden desks circling a black stove. Even the view from the schoolroom windows was drab. February gusts swung leafless branches of gray trees, and week-old snow covered miles of empty fields.

He looked at the pupils' faces, important with cleanliness, and a knot twisted inside his chest. He

tried to ignore it, not wanting them to expect anything but hard work from him.

Master Eaton had told him to begin each lesson
with a test. "Don't assume the older ones know the
most. Find out where each pupil stands and start
from there," the old man had counseled. And Will,
unsure of himself, frightened by the length of the
day ahead, knowing he had to start somewhere, followed the advice. Not until now did he realize a
teacher was sometimes less sure of himself and of his
knowledge than the pupils that sat before him.

Slowly, as the days went by, he began to know his
students. There was James Overton, so tall he
humped in his chair like a crescent moon; Beardsley,
whose eyes looked as though they had been scrubbed
to the bright blue that dominated his face. There
was the chubby one who pounced on his books as
voraciously as he gobbled his noon meal; the timid
boy trying to hide himself in the back of the room
behind his eyelids. But Will tried to be interested
only in the amount of resistance each offered his
teaching. In the third row, second seat, Robinson se-
creted himself behind a mask through mathematics,
logic, and grammar. Yet with any story, poem, or
play the mask shattered. Shakespeare, the Bible, Cae-
sar, — every teller of a tale could rouse him to pleasure, anger, fright, humor. The boy vibrated to the
subtlest innuendo. Week after week, Will groped for
a way to show him the precise beauty he himself
found in numbers and logic.

And Hansen, the farm lad, who manfully endured

each hour of lessons till he could get back to the life business of chopping wood, milking cows, working horses. He waited out the days as patiently as Mother Earth waited through that long Connecticut winter.

"How did the great Russian landowners achieve their power, Hansen?" Will asked.

The boy's face was blank as his first day's examination paper.

Will waited.

Seasons of waiting for seeds to take root, for plants to grow to maturity; years of time-biding till one pregnant cow became a herd, had bred patience in Hansen far beyond the schoolmaster's ken. Hansen sat. Will tapped his fingernails on his desk.

"Well?" the teacher demanded.

Every nerve in the room was alert to his irritation.

"Landowners are always rich. And rich men are powerful," interrupted Jenkins, the merchant's son, who couldn't bear the waiting either.

Hansen nodded in serious agreement.

"But why are landowners rich, Hansen?" Will insisted.

The boy answered as though he were talking to a demented child. "Grain grows on land. People need grain to feed their stock and themselves."

"All right. Now say each man starts out with the same amount of land —"

"But they don't. Intending no offense, sir, but where one man inherits a poor farm, another inherits a large one." He spoke slowly, trying to explain to the bookish master the simple way things are.

The teacher's obvious consideration of the answer barely suppressed titters that slipped through the room. Will's own laughter was stopped by the suspicion the boy was suddenly edging toward interest like a hunting dog catching a bare hint of scent. Impulses quickening, Will hurried, groping for a practical question to tempt the boy further. What? How could he put it? He felt the boy slipping back toward apathy. Go on. Catch him any way you can. "But you will admit there are a few men who start with an equal land portion?" He barely waited for Hansen to complete his nod.

"Say three in one county? The first man knows nothing about farming, thinks it merely a matter of planting seeds and waiting for them to grow. The second man is the son of a long line of Dutch farmers. He knows how to raise Dutch crops in Dutch soil under Dutch weather conditions. Though he finds himself in Connecticut, he's convinced that what was good enough for his father is good enough for him."

Hansen signaled his solemn approval of such a worthy thought.

Will clutched at the lad's interest with a return nod. "He'll use the old methods and *make* them work." He had the boy now. Still holding on, he rushed him toward certain disagreement, the one way Will had to reach his goal. "The third man has a similar heritage. But he's not afraid to change himself and his methods to suit the times. He sees that tobacco grows well, but he also reads the newspapers and realizes that because of an impending blockade any crop raised for export, despite the high price it might fetch in a foreign port, is a risky business. So he looks further and sees that corn, too, grows well, though it requires more labor to cultivate and the local price is fairly low. Still, he can sell part of it, and with the money buy a cow. He can store a portion of it to feed the cow, while his family eats the remainder and has butter, cheese and milk from the cow. He might even plant all his land in corn, but he knows if there is too much corn available the price will go down. So he plants three-quarters of his acreage in corn. One-half of that he plants in May, the other half he plants later and not as deep in the soil, to see which method produces a better crop. The remaining quarter of his acreage he gambles in tobacco. Now, after ten years of equally hard work, which of the three men will be able to buy more land?"

"Hard to say. There's still something to be said for the tried and true."

"Which one?" Will insisted.

He watched the boy, could almost feel the straining in his head, almost hear the thought rumbling in the solid New England rock of his mind. A small battle, Will knew, but whichever way the argument went, he had won. Hansen was thinking. For a second Will caught himself hoping it would not lead the young man to trouble. He had merely done his job. This was the risk Hansen's father ran when he sent him on to grammar school. Let them wrestle out the consequences. Despite that uncomfortable prospect, Will's spirits rose. He was a teacher.

His elation continued through the day, lifting him to one success after another. Walking home, he planned the next day's lesson, how he would keep Hansen thinking, move Beardsley on to Virgil, accelerate Robinson.

But a letter waited for him in his room. He saw it on the chest waiting, demanding his attention. Suddenly the swell of pleasure in him shriveled.

He put his books down slowly, postponing the moment he would open it. He moved toward the letter, looked at it, still didn't touch it. It was an intrusion, like an unwanted visitor who chooses the wrong moment to arrive. What right did Abigail have to barge into the new comfort of his life? Curse their invisible bonds. He wanted nothing to do with any of them. He wouldn't read the letter, not until he convinced himself nothing in it could affect him.

For three days it lay there, nagging at him even when he didn't see it. Finally fatigue more than conviction forced him to open it.

My dear Will'm,

How are you faring? Well, I hope. There has been no word from you though you said you would write. Your brother Sol'm and I were wondering (before he too left) but naturally you are all right or we would have heard different.

The house is very quiet. The only company we have is Abrh'm's seldom letters and a few more

*from Sol'm. As far as we know they are both well.
Sol'm happy to be appointed ensign.*

*Goods are short here, as everywhere, I suppose.
The butcher hasn't offered a roast of meat in three
months but with just the two of us and your father
barely touching his food it would be a waste to
cook anyways.*

*There is little to sell in the shop. People con-
tinue to ask for such they know we don't have and
your father spends most his day fighting the British from his chair and waiting the post that rarely
comes.*

*I hope you continue well and in his heart I
know so does your father.*

Your loving aunt,
ABIGAIL

He folded the letter, shut it out of sight, hoping he
could again shut them all out of his mind. It was so
much better the way it had been, separated from anger, warmth, pride, love, jealousy, wrath, tenderness.
Not knowing Abigail was worried about his father's
health, he hadn't thought of it. Now he must worry.
Nonsense, missing a few meals never hurt anyone.
Still —

He plowed back into his work, telling himself he
had neither time nor desire to answer the letter.
School was to continue through the summer, so those
who wished to graduate before joining the army
might do so. A few of the farm lads dropped out but

Will was glad enough to keep school for the others. He couldn't return to New Haven.

Throughout that summer and the next, into fall and now in the winter of '79, he was still in Groton, still hiding behind his books from Abigail's and Elizabeth's occasional letters. The British raids were reaching further up the coast. His father was mourning, refusing to eat. Still Will *did* not, *would* not, care.

He had several letters from Rebecca. By her accounts Newport was gay with British officers. She was dancing her way through the war. Most of the congregation had foolishly emigrated when these gentlemen came, but the synagogue was intact. She could not forget how much he had enjoyed the services. Was he coming back?

Back to what? Plainly the gentile British gentlemen were fine escorts, but hardly suitable marriage partners. Her attitude annoyed him. Anyway, to go back to Newport was to take a side, to acknowledge a Tory allegiance he could feel no longer. He'd have nothing to do with her or any of her life. He wanted no allegiance to anyone. He was his own man.

But the war pursued him. There was unrest in the air, there were rumors in the streets. He refused to read newspaper accounts of British atrocities. Yet he couldn't help hearing Danbury had been burned, Fairfield wasted, Norwalk destroyed. But New Haven was safe. They'd never get that far up the coast.

Uneasiness rippled into the schoolroom. It pulled

at his pupils till none of his efforts could entice them to study. Furious, Will piled work on them. They reacted as stoically as the sandbags that surrounded the public buildings. Will was determined that the school was one place the hated war would not invade. He fortified himself behind a wall of books and papers, and dared the war to break through.

Then, in June, Elizabeth's letter came. He read it, re-read it, and furiously tore it in half, in quarters, in eighths — the sharp rip of the paper pleased him. He clenched the bits and pieces into a ball and hurled it across the room. It landed under the chair. Will looked away from it. He would not believe what she wrote. But she had stormed his bastion, almost crumbled it.

Suddenly he was on his knees groping for the paper, smoothing each piece flat on the floor in front of him. Carefully he worked the letter like a puzzle and, stretching his fingers across the matched pieces, he read it again while each word seared his mind.

Master Eaton's cousin in Danbury had been killed in a Hessian raid, trapped in his house and burned to death. Elizabeth had found Master Eaton wandering, half-crazed, looking for the road to Danbury, saying he must make sure they had given his cousin a proper burial.

The Hessians had captured Robin Cowley, already wounded, and tortured him till he screamed for death. Girls and women were attacked. Everyone feared New Haven was next.

Jacob looked grim, strained to pathetic thinness.

Jonathan had been teaching her to use a rifle. Perhaps she had been wrong. Horrifying as war was, maybe it *was* best to face it and finish it, rather than protest what existed while it destroyed you.

He swept the pieces of the letter away from him and abruptly stood up. She's a fool. They'll never attack New Haven, never get that far. And if by some chance they do, surely the militia can stop them at Morgan Point or even West Haven. But if there aren't enough men to hold the fort at Black Rock — a wave of helplessness swept through him, sickened him to nausea. He trembled, aching to help them at home, to ease Jacob's burden, make sure Elizabeth nor Abigail had no need of a rifle, to comfort Master Eaton. But he could not leave now, not until the end of the term. And then what — return from the dead to haunt his father? No. He had enough of Jacob's pride in him to forbid his crawling back in fear, though it be fear for them. Besides, it will never happen. Why let a hysterical girl frighten him?

Still he wrote to Abigail, each day waited anxiously for the return post, asked for news of the war, waited, told himself it couldn't happen, waited, wrote again. Never. Not New Haven. Waited through a nightmare of endless time.

At last he held it, trembling ripped it open —

Dear William,
The attack is imminent. Abraham arrived home very tired from the defeat at Verplanck Point. We fear to have him go back too soon. Your father has

sent word to Sol'm but there has been no answer.
Abr'hm told me to write you. Come home, Wil-
liam. There is need of every man or boy who can
carry a rifle.

Your loving aunt,
ABIGAIL

Reading it, Will knew his family and Elizabeth
meant more than anything to him, far more than
Hansen, Overton and the other students. He'd leave
a note for the school overseers.

[Chapter XV]

THE ROAD WAS HARD with summer heat. For hours dust had clouded behind and before his horse. The particles caught in Will's throat, dried his tongue and parched his mouth. He licked his lips to soothe the cracks. The horse raced further into night, raced against the wind that filled British sails, the treachery of the Hessians, Jacob's infirmity, Abraham's exhaustion, time itself. In an agony of anger Will kicked the beast who carried him through darkness. A wolf bayed and he felt a tremor ripple through the mare's flesh into his own thighs. Go on, he urged, praying stamina into the horse's legs.

The air grew heavy. Pine trees held out stiff fingers of warning. Will shuddered, frightened of his own fear. He pressed through the mire of dense, sticky warmth. Every movement was a struggle against an invisible weight which muffled sound and stifled motion. They raced, not wanting the rain that would end the heat. A soundless spear lighted the sky, illuminated the glistening heat of the mare's body.

Go girl, keep trying. Tenderness for the horse's effort filled him. They pushed forward. Another flash of lightning and Will urged her further, waited for the thunder, wondered why it was so long coming. On, on, and finally the sound crashed through. Again light ripped the night, thunder roared, and still no rain. Bushes sagged, weighted trees reached up. Every muscle in his body strained forward and yet the pressure of surrounding stillness seemed to rob him of movement. His shirt clung to his back, his thighs stuck to the saddle, even the palms of his hands sweated. He willed himself on, bent low, kicked, urged, soothed, heard the dull hoof thuds and still felt suspended in time and space. The sky rumbled ferociously, churned itself in anger till a scream of answering wrath rose in Will, swelled in his throat, but cracked, impotent on his parched tongue. For a moment he thought they must be running in place.

And then it came. Big, hard, wet pellets of fury lashed him back to life. They stung at his face, arms, legs, whipped against his back. Even the mare seemed revived until the rage of the storm soaked them both to shivering. Cold set hunger gnawing in him. Rivulets ran into pools that turned the road into a thick sea of mud. He could feel the horse struggle against the weight of the road that stuck to her legs. Needles of rain pierced like a thousand pins at his eyes and his thin shirt was useless on his quivering body. Still they raced through the storm. Wet, cold, hungry, dirty, limp, they outdistanced it and kept on.

They galloped, relieved and panicked by approaching dawn. Exhausted, the mare stumbled, each breath now a miracle of endurance. "Just to the next house," Will whispered, and felt the effort of his own words. His arms ached, his back was locked in pain, and his legs trembled. She dragged through rolling fields, back into a thicket of woods. Still no sign of farm, no sight of house. Mud caked his shirt and hands, his throat and tongue swelled to aching. His belly gnawed hungrily at itself, clamored for a meal, while his muscles ached for a place to lie down.

He knew he must let the horse rest or find another. But there was no place, nothing in sight. In desperation he dismounted, took her reins, walked her, prayed a short respite might be enough. She hobbled, stumbled, finally fell into a mound of soft grass, and Will, weak beyond speaking, fell beside her.

He woke in a rush of sunlight, hunger and hope. The horse was standing, nibbling grass, waiting.

He rode, walked, rode again, walked in weariness that clouded his sight, knowing only that he must reach New Haven.

He traded her for food and bought the roan stallion. All was mixed in the nightmare of the next forty hours. The ride, the heat, the thirst, the darkness and daylight mixed in a mind that could only remember the fear of the worst horror, the sound of cannons as he entered New Haven.

They boomed, overpowering the street noises — the clatter of hooves and wagon wheels, the calls of peddlers, the peal of church bells. They smothered the sounds of life.

With every boom Will's anxiety grew. Was his father all right? And Abigail? How long had this been going on?

He brought the reins down sharply across the horse's neck. Fear mingled with excitement. It had been so long — two or was it three years since he'd seen them?

At last he was on State Street, his father's house seconds away. Soon. Soon. Soon.

He flung himself off the horse. His hands trembled as he tethered his mount to a post.

Somehow he got inside the door.

"Father," he blurted.

Instantly Jacob was in the passage.

Will *was* in his father's house, looking into his face, watching his lips part to form his name soundlessly, "William."

They fell into each other's arms.

A few minutes later Will realized his father was holding him upright. Embarrassed, he stepped back.

Abigail waited. Her eyes said more than Will could bear. He grabbed her, hugged her till she laughed, "Please, William. Please."

Smiling, Will turned to his father. "Where's Abe?"

Jacob stared at him.

"Where's Abe?" Will asked again. He fought the alarm that sounded in his brain.

Jacob looked away. He hesitated, then spoke almost harshly. "Abraham's been wounded. They're evacuating the fort at Black Rock. He's stranded there."

Abe. Hurt. He was too tired to fight belief. Oh, God. If it had to be one of them, why not Sol? But it was Abe, and there was only Will to save him. Will knew it and knew, too, he had to go.

Abigail's face went white. Her hand caught Jacob's arm. "You can't let him go. Don't you see he's sick tired? And just a boy. Seventeen."

"Eighteen in April," Jacob said softly.

"He's ill. Don't let him go, Jacob."

The old man was uncertain. "Perhaps —"

Will shook his head. "I'll need a horse."

"One son for your old age. Save one, Jacob."

"Solomon's not —" The boy couldn't finish. It was almost as though he had wished it.

"We've heard nothing. He'll be all right, please God."

"The horse?" Now he *must* go.

Abigail's eyes implored her husband.

"We can't leave him there," Will said gently.

Jacob nodded slowly. "No, we can't leave him there." Still nodding, he studied his son's face. Then once more his arms gripped tight around Will. "Go with God," he whispered fiercely.

[Chapter XVI]

IN THE DISTANCE a blur of sound boomed, heavy and muffled as the morning heat. Will rose and fell with the horse's body in a rhythm so familiar, so lulling, he began to feel he had never been anywhere but astride a loping animal. The road and trees were much like yesterday's, or was it the day before? He couldn't be sure, nor could he believe he was riding to war, so close to home. He felt his eyelids slip and knew it would be easy to fall asleep in the saddle.

The sounds grew, at first ahead of him, then to the side, now all around him. A musket cracked and Will whipped forward to a jar in the animal's pace. Suddenly he was awake. Closer, closer, a shell screeched. The horse screamed a terrified whinny. Will fought to hold her. He soothed her on into the roar of cannon. Noise burst against his eardrums. He could not see beyond the hill ahead, but the fort lay just below it. Frightened, the animal stumbled once, twice, a third time, and Will could not risk laming her. He'd need her later. He guided her to the roadside, quickly dismounted and led her into a thicket.

She was tied securely and out of sight. On foot he headed cautiously forward through the trees.

The sounds grew louder. He cupped his hands over his ears while an agonized scream like the shriek of an animal pierced their shelter. He could not shut out the noise. He had to go *on*.

Now he reached the top of the hillock. He was out of the sheltering trees. He threw himself down in the tall grass. It was still damp and silky soft beneath his body. A shell burst in the distance but its screech was so sharp Will ducked. There was a sudden hush. He raised his head. Beneath him the fort swam into focus and he caught his breath. It was the devil's likeness of a child's toy. Only this was real and bigger. So much bigger. Within its split-railed walls, tattered remnants of the patriot band still held. Several men crouched over a cannon, kept it firing. Others used their muskets. Will watched two men fall on ground already littered with bodies. Beyond the fort he could see the British and the Hessians swarming forward in a semicircle toward the fort. They were an army of hundreds, swollen and sure of victory.

A wave of nausea swept the boy. He didn't want to see this, to be part of this nightmare. Those weren't men down there, but beasts preying on one another. In the bright sunlight of this midsummer's day they had all gone mad. And his brother was caught among them while he lay here on the hill unable to move. He felt as though he were suffocating.

Coward! Wasn't that what he was?

He put his face into the grass and retched.

His breathing was still labored. His heart pounded. The panic held him. But now the revulsion that gripped his stomach and throat was gone, his head began to clear. Abraham is down there. Will called on every resource of his flesh and blood, brain and will, and found himself moving.

He was a man now, his father's strength fresh in him, and he must find the best way to reach the fort. There, that clump of trees to the left. Keep low, clear of the bullets. He had to push himself forward and hold back at the same time. Careful. Inch by inch. Cannon balls burst in front of him, ripping the earth. Shouts, screams, musket blasts pounded through the searing sunlight. Streams of sweat poured down his face, over his lids, clouding his sight. He brushed the back of his sleeve over his face. A trumpet blared. The redcoats were coming closer. All Will could think of was Abraham the day he had last seen him, tall, strong, his face flushed dark with the blood of the house of David — curse anyone who spilled that blood.

Grimly, Will forced himself into a low crouch and ran into the clump of trees, through its coolness, then out again into the white-hot sun.

Ten redcoats, or was it more, were trying to scale the fort's far wall. The Americans couldn't hold out much longer. Soon that back gate would open. Soon the patriots must retreat. And when they did they must do it quickly, each man carrying only his own rifle. The wounded *must* be left. But not Abraham. He would never leave Abraham to those Hessian mercenaries, even if he was — a thought struck cold terror in him, blotting out all feeling. Now he saw nothing — not the scorched brown grass of the hillside, not the limp leaves of the trees. Sound was too loud, too constant to hear.

There was just one thing now — the fort. Two hundred rods to go. He crept and slid, half running, half stumbling.

And then it happened. The retreat began.

William stood up and ran forward. He no longer cared about the gunfire.

"Here, boy, don't go in there. The redcoats will be inside in minutes," a hoarse voice shouted.

William didn't answer. He mustn't waste breath or strength explaining. On. Go on. Through the gate.

Then he was inside the yard. He choked back a gasp and felt tears hot on his face. He had to look. The dirty bloody bodies lay where they had fallen. Some groaned and thrashed against their pain. A few were dignified by blankets. Others lay exposed in twisted silence. Abraham. O God of my fathers, Jesus or Jehovah, whatever your name, help me find your son Abraham. Lead me. Help me. He prayed unconsciously. He walked around buildings, behind them. Once he turned over a man lying face down in the dirt. A gaping chest wound oozed life. The man reached toward Will. For a second the boy stood, breathed the sick sweet stench of death, and forced himself on. There! Slumped over a cannon. Oh, God, let him be alive.

"Abe," he whispered.

His brother opened his eyes. "You came." A pained smile distorted his face. His eyes closed.

A British soldier dropped over the wall not fifty feet from them. Then another.

It was then William saw his brother's wound. The flesh of his upper thigh had been ripped ragged. Blood still trickled onto the bruised skin and stained the leg of his breeches with spreading darkness. Abe's face was gray as the dusty cannon, but the pulses in his temples throbbed. William leaned over him, pulled at his sleeve, whispered hoarsely into his ear, finally slapped his face, but could not evoke another flicker of life. Despair clutched at the boy's throat. Fear told him it was impossible to move Abraham, but his mind, pursued by panic, raced to seize any possibility.

He must go out the way he had come in — the back gate. Any minute the front portico would be open to swarms of victory-drunk redcoats and the other exit would be blocked, too. William sucked in his breath sharply, then swiftly bent low to raise Abraham to his shoulder. His nerves taut, his back muscles straining against Abraham's full weight, he began to rise. He tottered and staggered, his thighs trembled. A warm, thick wetness spread slowly over his back and he knew the bleeding had begun again.

Fear and blind instinct forced him forward on his hands and knees.

Will slumped forward until one shoulder almost touched the ground. Now he managed to press himself up against Abraham until he stood straight. The heat was so intense it seemed as though he had to push against it as well as against Abe's weight. Somehow he was behind the building and for an instant he leaned against it. The rough boards struck sharply into his arm and darkness hovered against the sides of his eyes. For what seemed an eternity he stood motionless, unable to move either foot. But at last it began again — the slow creeping, the groping.

Each step was an agony of effort. Left. Right. He could not look down, but only sightlessly ahead. Now something hard and sharp underfoot. He stumbled. And then he was down beneath the suffocating heat weight of his brother's body.

For a second he lay still. The victorious screams of the entering troops sliced into his consciousness. He forced himself up. An idea sent new strength coursing through him. Quickly he bent and removed Abraham's belt, wrapped it around his own chest, under his armpits, and buckled it behind his back. He took off his belt and hooked it to Abraham's. Using his own as a tow, he heaved.

Abe moved forward, slowly, very slowly. A few more rods to the end of the building, then five feet through the open space to the back gates. The shouts were closer now, and steps ran threateningly near. William hauled, tugged, and dragged at Abraham, fighting to deafen himself to the sound of his brother's pain. The leather belt cut into his fingers and knife-like stabs slashed at his chest. A miracle of perseverance brought him to the edge of the building. Wild hope hammered exultantly through him. He turned back to Abraham.

And then he saw the redcoats, not five feet from him. There were two of them, black leather straps shining against the hated red of their coats.

Will slipped down beside his brother and wept.

⌈ Chapter XVII ⌉

MERCIFULLY, Abe had fallen asleep.
Will lay still, so close to the soldiers' boots he
felt the ground's vibration and smelled the dust they
raised. He knew the men were looking for prisoners,
had found two in the main yard, and now would look
behind the barracks. He flung his arm over Abe,
stretched his hand across his brother's mouth and
buried his own face in the dirt.

If Abe should move or utter the slightest sound —
he tried to will silence into him and held his own
breath till his head swam.

"Any here?" The heavy voice seized him in a vise
of horror.

A boot prodded his hip. Will's body locked. Terror gripped his joints. The boot pushed harder. His
flesh became a rock of stubbornness. He felt the soldier's foot rise, heard the slash of air, the thump that
sent pain shrieking through his leg.

"Nein. This one will do the General no good."

Another swipe seared his thigh.

"No good left."

Will's heart drummed. If they should touch Abe — the possibility brought the taste of hate into his throat and sickened him. Touch his brother and he'd tear out their throats.

Go, his mind screamed.

"This one's finished, too."

Go.

"The General will not be happy."

The sun beat down, scorching body and brain, burning an invitation to the tiny black flies that buzzed about Will's ears and eyes. They lighted on the back of his neck, crawled inside his shirt, flew into his nose, stirring him toward frenzy. He dug his nails in his palm.

The guttural accents of the mercenaries grated against his ears. The sound was ugly and their laughter, sifted through his pain, became maniacal. Time was his only weapon.

His leg throbbed and the earth spun under him. He clawed at the earth. The Hessian voices faded, but he no longer trusted his senses. Perhaps they still stood sneering above him. Perhaps their silence was a trick. He waited, holding to consciousness with tremendous effort.

Time hung suspended from a sky that refused to darken. He heard no sound, felt no presence, but fear made him cautious. They've gone, reason assured him. Perhaps reason, too, was a trick.

Slowly, almost imperceptibly, the sun's heat edged toward retreat. Unsure, incapable of belief, he waited until he could no longer bear waiting. He raised his head, waited again. Nothing happened. Now he raised higher, and finally he turned. They were gone. The sun reached westward — another half hour, one hour at the most until dark.

He and Abe were alone except for a few blanketed bodies around them. He would wait until dark to attempt escape. But how? Surely the redcoats would never leave the exit unguarded. He scanned the fort wall — it was at least twelve feet high. Still *they* had scaled it. But he had Abe to carry and no rope ladder like they had used. Yet there was a way, had to be one. He only needed to find it.

He searched his mind, raced within it, ignoring the sounds of roistering that were beginning in the yard.

Abe moaned, but did not open his eyes. His breathing was regular and a hint of color showed along his cheeks and lips. A pulse of hope pumped excitedly in Will. His mind grabbed at it, held fast, and rushed to a solution.

As soon as it was dark he would take the blankets from the bodies, tie them together, then throw a loop around one of the wall's top spikes and hoist Abe up.

His mind whirled in a fever of details. Each one, carefully thought out, fired him to the next. His body tingled with tremors of possibility.

The raucous yard sounds heightened. The redcoats were drinking to their super-strength, super-acumen, super-general, laughing uproariously at their super-wit and Will barely heard them. The crackle of a bonfire began in the yard. He couldn't wait until dark.

He crept toward the barracks, slithered along the ground and wondered how much longer his body could respond to his commands. Still he inched forward, reached out, took hold of the corner of a blanket and slid it toward him. Then another and another till he held three covers beneath him.

Refusing to look at the men whose last dignity he stole, he crept back. Just a few rods to go, but his leg burned with a shaft of pain. As he fell down next to Abe, it speared his body. In the twilight he lay listening to a man's screams for mercy, and heard only the bedlam of his own fright.

At last he could sit up. He began to knot the blankets together.

He did not know how long Abe had been awake. He only knew his brother had wakened and now watched him.

"How is it?" Will whispered.

Abe moved his lips, but there was no sound. He tried again. "I — don't have — strength. Won't make it."

Will caught the sob in his throat. "Yes. You will, you will."

Abe shook his head. "Wait until dark. Then you go."

"I can't. Not without you."

"Yes, go."

"Abe, I can't leave you," he motioned his head toward the yard but meant the screams.

Abe's eyes filled. "Please, Will, I have no strength left to try. Let me be. Why should two of us die?"

Will stood up. It was dark now. He pulled at each knot, tested it against his own strength. He found a stone and tied it securely in the end of the blanket. Now he retested his work.

He glanced toward the barracks. All clear.

"I'm going to tie you in before I throw it," he whispered to Abe.

Abe nodded.

He was lashed in securely. One last look around. Will's first toss caught by a miracle. The rest was a race. Every passing second, every sound, was a threat. Will climbed first, swayed, climbed further, heard wood crack, climbed on, finally wedged himself between the spikes and gripped the wall with his thighs. He could see the bonfire and the soldiers sprawled about it. If one of them should look up —

"Hold on, Abe. I'm going to pull you," he whispered as loudly as he dared.

He couldn't see below him, but he heard Abe groan and at the same moment, felt the blankets grow taut. His own legs trembled. He leaned out, bracing himself against Abe's weight.

Holding on with his legs, he pulled on the blanket with one hand while he wrapped it around the other. It cut into his wrist, blocked the circulation from his hand, but he held on. Slowly Abe moved upward. Then he, Will, was sliding, pulled inward over the wall. Desperately he hugged the spikes with his thighs. Wood splinters cut through the cloth of his breeches into his skin.

Suddenly the line went limp. Will teetered backward. Trembling, he sought his balance and looked down.

"Sorry. Had — to let — go," Abe whispered. Lying there suspended in the blanket halter, he seemed too tired to care.

"Try, try, try," Will urged.

Abe barely shook his head.

"I'll come down and get you."

"Not sure this blanket will hold us —" His words trailed off. His eyes closed.

Clutching at the top spikes, Will jumped free of the wall, caught the blanket around his good leg, wrapped it as far as it would go, and with every ounce of his remaining strength raised his leg. Every muscle in his body cried out as he pulled. Inch by inch Abe moved. Now the spikes cut into Will's hand. It was warm with his own blood and still he held. He would have to reach down with one hand to raise Abe the rest of the way. Carefully he eased his right hand away from its hold. Searing pain pulled through his left arm, pried at his fingers. He swayed, but jammed his wrist between the slats and stifled a cry.

Then, sickened with dizziness, he screamed, "I can't hold. I'm letting go." In a superhuman effort, Abe reached up, caught at the blanket and relieved the pull.

An uproar spread through the yard. The soldiers had heard Will's cry. But in that second Abe and Will were up and over, sliding down the other side. Crawling, running, limping, dragging until they were astride the waiting horse.

Chapter XVIII

WILL WOULD NEVER remember the trip back. The night was the noise of cannon, musket, air ripped by racing horse and man, pounding hooves and pulses. War followed them into the town, filling it with the terror of invasion. And finally, incredibly, they were on State Street, then inside Jacob's house and blessed stillness.

Will soaked in it, sucked at it hungrily. Slumped in a chair beside the kitchen hearth, he forced himself to swallow a long draught of the steaming rum Jacob held to his lips. A wave of nausea, then quick heat coursed through his veins. Once more his father lifted the mug. Another sip and Will could raise his head.

Abe lay on the kitchen table, his face pain-white, while Abigail's fingers worked surely and quickly at his wound. Her face showed no fear. So calm she could not fail to comfort, she moved from boiling kettle to cloth to wound.

Jacob had sent a messenger to fetch the doctor. Until he could be found and brought back, it was Abigail and her pots and home-brewed elixirs and strips of torn sheeting who must ease Abe's hurt and urge the color back into his face.

Comfort flowed from her unsought, as surely as breath, as unremarkable. Watching her, Will knew tenderness so keen it pushed tears against his eyes. He mustn't let them fall. Not yet. There was one more thing he must do tonight.

"My musket, it's here, isn't it? We have powder, don't we?" he asked his father.

"You're not going out now? You mustn't. You're too tired. Besides, there'll be no more fighting tonight."

"I can see the captain tomorrow. Right now I have a different errand."

His father moved toward him. "William." He was down beside him, his arms were around him. His shoulders trembled. "I don't want you to join."

There was fear in Jacob's voice. Shocked, Will stiffened. His own fright surged up to meet his father's. But a new strength in him squelched it and made his tone soothing. "I have to join. But tomorrow. And I'll come back. Bring Sol with me, too."

Still holding Will's shoulders, Jacob leaned back to look at him.

Then spilling into his father's face came all the warmth and respect and love for which Will had yearned.

There was no more, no wish for more, between the two men.

Will closed his hand around his father's arm, then rose. "I'll be back as soon as I can." He didn't have to wait for Jacob's nod.

Hurriedly he closed the door behind him. He must make sure Elizabeth was safe. Then he could rest.

The gunfire had stopped, but sound still filled the street. Voices shouted orders. Half-sleeping children cried. Overburdened wagons clattered by. The road north was jammed, the escape road.

"The redbacks'll be in New Haven by noon and no mistake."

"Johnny Tompkins dead."

"They burned Fairfield. They'll never let New Haven stand."

"Get the women out."

He ran. Elizabeth. On and on. Another half mile. His mind willed but his legs were unsteady. On and on till he could see the Brookley house, which blazed with light.

The door was open and there she was, moving with Abigail's sureness among the wounded men that lay on couches, tables, stretchers, and lined the floor in demanding rows.

Her dress and face were streaked, her sleeves rolled up to her elbows. Strands of red-gold curled limp with sweat about her face.

Women, too old to escape, and girls, too frightened, scurried to Elizabeth's orders. Jonathan carried a kettle of boiling water too carefully for his bobbing gait to spill. Will took the cauldron from him and handed it to the pock-marked woman who beckoned.

"Jonathan," Will said, "the redcoats'll overrun the town by morning. You've got to get her out."

"My father took Mother to her sister in Killingsworth. He left me to bring Liz as soon as she'd finished here, but she won't —"

Will didn't listen further. Suddenly he was remembering the awful curse she had flung at him — "burn for the Jews' everlasting guilt. Burn in hell." Words hurled in fear and anger, forgiven now. Forgiven completely and surely as his father and he had forgiven each other words no less cruel.

He stepped over and around the wounded. She was on her knees, wiping a face inflamed by fever. He grabbed her arm and pulled her upright. "Go with Jonathan. Get out of New Haven. Now."

Her eyes filled. "Thank God you're safe." But she went back to the wounded man.

Once more Will pulled her up. "Elizabeth, it's not your fight. Remember?"

She shook her head. "I didn't want it, but now it's mine and it's Jonathan's. Besides, Master Eaton can't be moved and is helpless without us. We must stay and do everything we can. You go, Will. When it's over I'll tell you how wrong we were not to —"

"I know. I know." He felt her hand in his, knew suddenly and fully the dearness of her. "Tomorrow I'm going to join the army, but I want to know you're safe."

Her eyes, tawny gold and green as he remembered, held his. "And I want to know you're safe, but we can't know that, either of us. It's all part of it."

She was right and he was helpless knowing it. She had grown, too.

"Liz —" his voice shook.

"Yes, Will, I know."

Of course she knew. But when the war was won he would tell her anyway.

[*Author's Note*]

William Pinto did go on to fight with the Revolutionary Forces. When General Arnold arrived at Fort Trumbull, Will was given the honor of carrying the news to
the Governor. At the war's end, all three brothers returned safely to New Haven. Solomon Pinto was elected
to the Society of Cincinnati, General Washington's se-
lect group of valiant soldiers.

These facts, Jacob Pinto's contribution to the American fight for freedom, the brothers' attendance at Yale
College, Will's copies of the Declaration of Independence and his daring rescue of his brother Abraham, were
the basis for this otherwise imaginary story.

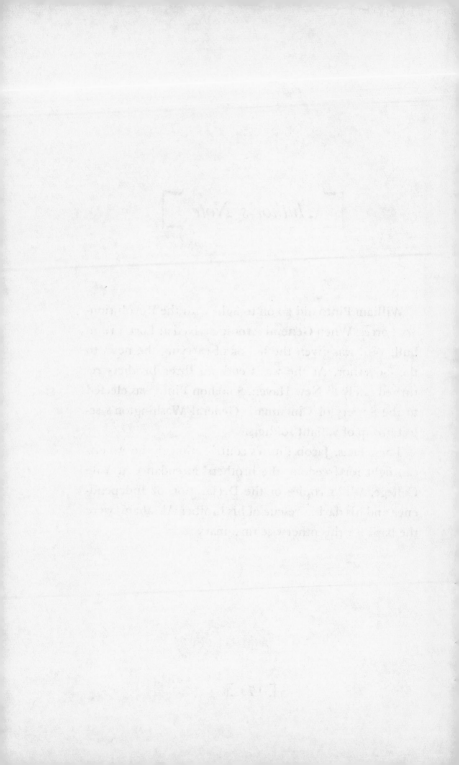

Date Due

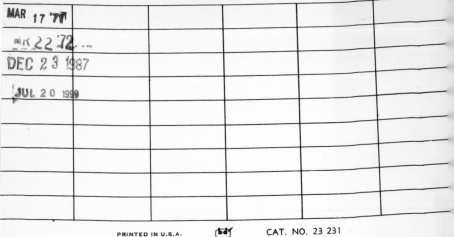